Brinley
Maggie:
my all you ✓
corry
be clear

Realizing that the skills that he obtained from Barry University in 1988 while studying Communication Arts were important in daily life, Marc O'Brien decided to take his trade in a whole new direction. Living in Las Vegas O'Brien has put together a strong portfolio of fictional works that challenge the reader to interpret and learn from his writings. Blue Note Publishing were the first to bring his thoughts to the public when they assisted O'Brien through self-publishing *Peter The Peteeatrick Panda's Playground*, *Peter The Peteeatrick Panda and the Pandy Chip Pancakes* and *A Special Person To Ride.*

Dedication

This work is dedicated to the pony, an educator who does not judge a book by its cover, instead fills its pages with lessons that a child can interpret and understand.

Marc O'Brien

THE FINAL FENCE

Sophomores in the Saddle

AUSTIN MACAULEY PUBLISHERS™

LONDON • CAMBRIDGE • NEW YORK • SHARJAH

A CIP catalogue record for this title is available from the British Library.

ISBN 9781788233538 (Paperback)
ISBN 9781788233545 (Hardback)
ISBN 9781788233552 (E-Book)
www.austinmacauley.com

First Published (2018)
Austin Macauley Publishers Ltd™
25 Canada Square
Canary Wharf
London
E14 5LQ

Acknowledgments

This unique story could not have come about if it was not for the English riding world educating me with equitation skills which can be translated into proper social skills. From the classroom perspective it was Middletown High School South that prepared me for what Barry University had in store for me.

As for the reader I would like to let you know this book is a springboard for reflection and interpretation. It is a work of fiction and winning is not the important factor in the story, instead it's living. So sit back, relax and take my course that I designed in *The Final Fence: Sophomores in the Saddle.*

THIS IS NOT A BOOK
ABOUT HORSES.
THIS IS NOT AN INSPIRATIONAL
TALE OF COMMITMENT;
INSTEAD, IT IS OUR STORY ABOUT
WHAT WE DEDICATE OUR HONEST AND
SUPPORTIVE LOVE TO.

In the Beginning
There Is Always a Conflict That Comes Down
To the Last Obstacle

Peter King still laid out the artistic journalistic statement in the same manner as he did when the college information center was the editor's scholarship job that paid his way through the International University. Funny how working for the National Weekly Newspaper, he still kept his creative juices alive in pounding out country club tidbits then distributing the credible forming items to the masses who the advertisers thought read the unique style of concise scripture that was written in a fashion that was comfortable to the reader.

Advertisers were funny, the thirty-year-old thought, picking up the latest department store pitch featuring a lady in a bikini, *looks get things noticed.*

Then it came off the wire in a short-paragraphed press release from an unknown media outlet, but the New York dateline captured his eye before he attached the scotch tape to the back.

Century-Old Horse Show Gets Nixed at Corporate-Owned Arena

Geezus, Peter thought out loud to himself while admiring the beauty of the athletic image, *this was what the northerners used to love to do when they lived down here.*

Peter could remember being a student reporter watchdog trucking the camera and notebook out to the Sunshine State Fair Ground's to do photo-ops of Eddie Patrick and Danielle Lynne's social sporting exhibition.

From a picture taking standpoint, the sporting day-long competition seemed to be very tranquil, unlike the other Division 2 spectacles that attracted a handful of Southern Dominican Catholic students to the recreational as well as therapeutic outlets that were an escape from the books. In fact, the equine events were easy to cover while the stories seemed to challenge his senses, creating something that was sensational and not hurtful to anybody.

Seeing the tragic story reminded him about all the good times they had in the social atmosphere inside and outside the classroom as they were following their youthful dreams, which in the end finished with them understanding the definition of the word 'goals'.

Southern Dominican Catholic University had a philosophy about education: instead of attacking it straight on, they would sneak up behind the young adults by letting them figure it out for themselves through proper decision making and, in some cases, prayer.

"In other words, here is the material," the Sisters who dressed in casual clothes would say, "here is the information, now learn."

Peter chuckled while inserting the horse story next to the bikini model advertisements.

Looking down at the artistic and journalistic statement that debated public relations through marketing, the local reporter stood there in remembrance of those days when innocence was married to honesty.

Knowing that he was finished for the week, Peter put the news-worthy item that was in a layout form in a circular canister, labeled the package followed by a stamp, and then dropped it in a bin to go to the main office somewhere in another state.

On his desk, the red lights read 1:45 in the morning and the only thing open at this hour was Denny's, and Peter was not ready to deal with the man beast, not tonight anyway; instead, it was off to bed then two days off.

"Well, sort of," he could hear himself speak, shutting the lights and door, "yes, Eddie Patrick, the cripple from the Garden State that had two first names. Boy, did he bring peace to this county, or really two counties."

Somewhere in a Rural Area of the Garden State

Danielle Lynne saw memories counted in many years as she viewed the tack room, trying to get the final chores done before moving to the South to attend college. For fourteen years, she had an education inside the stable that seemed very challenging but never really related to the books that were in the classroom. Instead, the horses were like teachers while the Equine Scholastic Aptitude tests lived up to their names by testing everyone at the same time. Unlike the structured exams that they had at the local high school, the preppie brunette-haired equestrian's life was the show-ring, which gave positive grades to the student who kept her face in the texts when not on course.

Remembering facts, dates, and speeches really was not the elegant seated hunter's/jumper's specialty, who still had dreams to ride at a plateau which would bring her to a successful peace. It never dawned on her about the politics since her main love was the horses and being able to understand their minds, while working together to achieve a goal.

Show jumping continued to have a magical aspect that could be classified as a first-class romantic excursion for the spectator filled with entertaining and athletic exhibitors, capturing the competitive eye with a natural visual experience. Love for Danielle Lynne was not a four lettered word; instead, it was John who just seemed to be there like a bridle that hung on the hooks above her head. Yes, he was just an apparatus she would grab a hold of when needed and after the use it gets cleaned up, placed with care until the next time the leather piece is needed.

Her real devotion was the chestnut mare that was being loaded into the trailer for her trip down to *County Line Stables* on the border of the two counties that encompass South Florida. Built to change riders into winners, the unique training ground had some amazing talent, making the show grounds into a centerpiece for respectability. It was owned by her Uncle Nate, and it was going to be nice to get to him after all the years learning the trade in the northeast. Also, there was Southern Dominican Catholic University an hour down the road from the facility which, in true honesty, was the reason behind the move. With one year's community college under her belt, it was time to make a commitment to a four-year school so she could have something to fall back on when the Equestrian goals were not able to be pinned.

All of a sudden, Danielle Lynne heard screams from the tack room, so she peered from outside in a curious way. She could see the mice scurrying around, trying to strategically eat their way into the feed room. A couple young lead liners were all so petrified that their actions made her laugh about the horror stories that her dad used to tell inside the barn when they were trying to clean the tack.

Cleaning the equipment might be chores for many but Danielle Lynne used to relish in the experience. Since it was so quiet, it gave her time to think and even dream. The Jersey Girl thought a realistic achievement would be to see Europe in the saddle and have her companion, 'The Great Satan', underneath her guiding the excursion. For all her teenage years, the talented individual was able to go through the northeast and see where all the British and French colonies were located back in the day. Their rebellious style against the colonial power base made her activity a visual masterpiece, colored with beauty that glorified the elegant time.

John, who was Danielle Lynne's four lettered word, rode up on a Harley and popped off as the helmet went on one of the handlebars. He knew she was just going through the flows and the day finally came when their post high school relationship was splitting up due to reality. He was not blaming her parents for sending her down to Florida, claiming a new horse training center as an excuse, ready to make another business move. The rose in John's hands really was a going-away present along with a good luck message. By the time the holidays rolled around, she figured there would be another girl ready to enjoy his company.

"Hello, John," Danielle Lynne stated, wiping the gookety gook from her hands that developed while giving her saddle one last wipe down using the greasy-like substance which made the leather shine.

"Hi, Danielle," was his response, trying to recapture a memory with the smell.

"Heading off to school tomorrow, I see," the disruption announced.

Feeling uncomfortable and not wanting to hurt him in any way, she confirmed the question with a nice hug and a peck on the cheek.

"Yep, I arrive in sunny South Florida tomorrow and The Great Satan will be there in two days, which gives me time to unpack in my dorm."

"Just wanted to give you this rose as a happy parting, last night's dinner was really special."

She took it from him with a show jumping smile, in a way that it did mean something, but still, John was just the four letters always there whenever Danielle Lynne needed a companion to get her through a vent full situation.

Watching his package make its way back to his bike and turning around like a school teacher in front of the class, the now sophomore in college could see the lead liners watching the episode unfold like a soap opera tragedy on television.

"All right, you little chair ups, back to work."

"Yes, Miss Danielle," half of them quietly retorted while the other portion in the same tone expressed knowing that in a few hours Miss 'perfect diagonal led counter canter' will be somewhere else giving them peace. "Yes, Miss Lynne."

Chuckling, they all returned to their own responsibilities with the knowledge that in a few hours Ms. Perfect Equestrian will no longer sit there at the rail screaming, 'You are on the wrong diagonal,' or lead when all they were doing was hacking in the ring. Not schooling!

Schooling was so much different than hacking. You had to be on the proper diagonal, you had to jump the fence in the number of strides that the judge sitting on the rail in a conversation wanted you to count, and finally, all the tack had to be perfect, while the clothes all needed to look perfect, since Miss 'blue ribbon' Danielle Lynne was around to give the white glove treatment.

Of course, hacking the rules was almost the same, but they looked good when everything came together, so the critical words during training really did not matter. There were times when these 'little munchkins', as Miss Danielle Lynne called them, would question whatever happened just to going out and enjoying being with the one you loved, giving the partner a hundred percent attention without everything being a major production.

Danielle Lynne came to the row of stalls and the chestnut mare was resting on four legs, nibbling at the hay the kids neatly threw over the door with the pitchfork.

"The Great Satan," she said, noticing the nylon halter with the scripted gold name-plate, "we did real well in juniors, now it is time to go for the big stuff."

With a stable built to design respectability, North/South County Line Stables was going to be a new landmark on the South Florida Equestrian scene that included Palm Beach and Wellington competing for tourists with the rest of South Florida.

"Yes, Great Satan, they have the best weather down there and with all year round perfection, the degree is not the only thing I plan on getting."

Turning around, she could see the kids all dressed in britches and boots, holding their mounts in one hand while studying the course, contemplating how many strides were needed in between each obstacle. They were playing horse show with imaginary mounts just like their brothers would pretend being Yankees at the big stadium in the Bronx. Keeping in mind the information they were fooling around with was instilled in their minds, like a date on a history test.

"Soon they will be juniors and that will be a magical time for them," Danielle Lynne smiled, watching the innocent learn the basic lessons behind strides between fences and preparing for things in a way that they will be able to overcome any obstacle in clean fashion.

15 Miles to the Rest Stop

As the sun peaked out of the early cloudy day, the radio crackled with WNEW-FM and Eddie Patrick paid the toll by giving the New Jersey Turnpike manila ticket along with a green piece of paper.

The Delaware Memorial Bridge and two days later I will be back home, he said to himself, leaving the Garden State in his rearview mirror and with Southern Dominican University dead ahead.

Driving through the depressing, cloudy early morning air the light blue 'Welcome To Delaware' sign passed by without any fanfare, while the multi-colored rest stop announcement came closer, giving notice to all the different places that visitors could use as an excuse to pull off the highway that charged a fee.

Unlike Maryland, the smallest state had the same work alcoholic presentation at its fast-food roadway court. Get them in, get them out; as quick as possible. Believe it or not, only a few miles down the Interstate after the state line, there were more comfortable places to stretch legs and the tourists did seem to have a relaxing feel instead of the business oriented 'there is no time to stop' attitude. After this brief introduction to rural driving, the tie ups before the historical landmarks were a quick reminder to the fact the final cosmopolitan region will be the last true hellish slow down until the Southern Florida area. After engaging in this beltway controlled madness for an hour, the true Southern Hospitality replaced the solo driver's mindset, making the endurance test an exit to exit challenge.

Eddie pondered pulling off, but once again, a good song came over the crackled radio, and the time to eat was put off until the next thirty miles and the Maryland House.

Should be Flying High in the Friendly Skies

"Now, Danielle Lynne," the voice could be heard as the equestrian picked at the donut that was getting a suntan from the bright light that was being beamed from outside the large window at the dull-looking Newark Airport.

As her father just smiled, Danielle Lynne chuckled.

"Now, Danielle Lynne, The Great Satan is fine, they are already in North Carolina and will be at the farm by sundown today," he assured his daughter about her pride and joy.

"I am going to miss you but it is going to be an interesting experience."

"Yes, Danielle Lynne, Southern Dominican Catholic University is a fine, fine school," the mother explained, "when I went there it was just a girl's school but now it is a major university."

"Well, I am sure looking forward to it."

"Have you talked to your new roommate?"

"She is returning to Southern Dominican Catholic University as a nursing student."

Checking his watch, the Father noticed it was time to head to the gate. Danielle Lynne brushed the white dust off her preppie-looking sweater that made her look like a dead ringer for someone from a middle class northeast household.

The trio marched to the brown-and-orange hallway.

"Okay, Dad, you have to get back to the city and your work in the Trade Center. I can handle it from now."

"Danielle Lynne, think of college as a journey filled with many different situations."

"You mean an excursion through hell," Danielle Lynne quipped, remembering all the things she had to work out during this South Florida trip.

"No, Danielle Lynne, it is like the jumper courses you do with The Great Satan: each fence is a class, some are difficult than others, but then when you finish and look back at the ring, what is done is done and what is learned is learned."

Giving them both a hug, Danielle Lynne, the owner of the show jumper The Great Satan, broke away with the comment, "That orientation class better not be a triple combination."

"It isn't, but the eight in the morning math class not only has a wide spread, but the water makes it a real bitch on a Friday morning," her father chuckled, knowing paying her education's entry fee would be a good investment.

Laughing, Danielle Lynne headed down the hallway, dropping her Walkman in the container and continuing to give the security guards her preppie, innocent collegiate look.

Since nothing rang or buzz, they wished her a safe travel, prompting her to pick up the earphones with a tape deck inside containing John Parr's Greatest Hits with a special selection from Phil Collins. Danielle Lynne saw the silver mechanical bird sit, waiting like a horse inside a stall ready to be boarded, with the lettering 'Piedmont' on its side. She knew it was time to leave New Jersey and face her new challenges in this competition called 'life'.

Exit to Sleep

It was seven hours after Eddie filled his tank at the historical welcome center and with Georgia's state line in reach, the late summer sun still had a couple hours left to its day despite the bright-yellow ball starting to be a dangerous destruction. Every couple miles, a motor inn anchored the roadway to nowhere and with a diner eatery in its parking lot, the business gold mine seemed an important place for him.

Coming to a complete stop in the parking lot, Eddie took advantage of the blue marking spaces denoting the handicap logo. It was the twentieth anniversary when he was born disabled, and ever since he had the car, the wider places to pull into were a nice safety valve in crowded areas.

Eddie used to think to himself why these actually needed to exist, why should they be there? Was it a right for him to be able to park so close to where he was going? Why should he be going there in the first place?

Deciding to let those thoughts go, he shut over the white door, brought down the two canes off the roof, and started to walk like a dog or horse, one leg at a time.

When he reached the bell desk, a man came into view, asking him how he could help.

"I have a reservation, Patrick, Eddie Patrick," the adult said in a mature voice.

"Yes, Patrick, Eddie Patrick, here it is: Room 2 on the first floor, it has handicap accessibility."

There was that word again: handicap accessibility. Why did they have to make sure all the rooms were accessible to the handicapped? This establishment was meant to get a few winks of sleep with all the bathrooms having showers that were used for in-out and on your way.

Once again, Eddie threw those thoughts into the back of his mind and took the keys along with the luxury to Room 2 on the first floor.

Parental Guidance

"Dad, for the last time, if you do not start eating right this stuff will kill you. I have got to get over to school to get my room settled and classes registered," Bobbi Barnes said, wearing her nursing uniform with the 'Southern Dominican Catholic University' patch on the right arm.

"Honey, I know you love me but these are so good and they are good for you. Here, try some."

"Eeegh, Gaad, it is so greasy."

"Do you need the check for the school?"

"Yes, Daddy, they want things up front just in case we disappear after the first class."

Mr. Barnes signed his name on the rectangular piece of paper and handed it over to his only daughter who was entering her second year as a nursing school at the private university. She looked so much like her mother he couldn't stand it.

"When is Mom coming home? Tell her I am thinking about staying in the dorm tonight since my new roommate is moving in today."

"Good, since without you around, we can have a peaceful night and probably go out for dinner."

"Well, I will see her at the hospital tomorrow when we have our introduction to a hospital floor for the first time."

"Well, I have got to go," Bobbi said to her father, giving him a hug, "and stay away from that greasy fat."

Once again Mr. Barnes chuckled as his daughter headed out the door looking like a professional in a field that boarded motherhood. And in a sense, she was just here to look over a group of patients on a floor then walk away, giving them each special attention until turning off the lights and heading back to her life.

Chasing a Cloud

Danielle Lynne watched the water crash onto the famed Fort Lauderdale beaches that were thousands of feet below her as she looked out the window in the mechanical tube designed to allow people to move long distances in a short time period.

Taking the cut carrots and apples out of the plastic bag, she made the commitment to herself that it was time to make this move work. Taking her mind off the new area that she was being shipped to for boarding purposes, the talented equestrian went back to the horse magazine she was reading over and over, cover to cover. But at this magical glance, she came across a story she missed in her previous engagements with the publication.

The headline read:

Disabled Horseman Takes Gold in Michigan Games

As she read the account about the horseman from her state, the reading expedition allowed her to learn that there was a guy out there who not only loved horses but respected them honestly.

"We will be landing at the Fort Lauderdale International Airport in a few minutes," the loudspeaker crackled, giving Danielle Lynne preparation to come out of the clouds.

Traveling Through Time

The television crackled with a boxing movie about an Italian in red-and-white shorts. Eddie Patrick watched it, remembering how inspirational the film's final message was on the impact that one person's support can have on a person's successes.

It was the first time Eddie looked at the sweat bands that donned both his wrists, thinking back to himself that it must be nice to have that true unattainable feeling that comes when the protagonist gets after the credit-rolling scene. He watched the protagonist get a hug from his leading lady as the upbeat musical score distributed the information about the sports fantasy.

Only five years ago, the athletic wear covered the mistake Eddie made during a fall weekend when things seemed so desperate that even the possible was impossible. Unlike the William Shakespeare tale, there was no leading lady to bring the house to tears; instead, it was a tragic Thanksgiving reunion which in reality was not his in the first place.

Dressed in a sports jacket and tie bearing a colorful pattern that really had no bearing except to match the shirt along with the rest of the ensemble, Eddie decided his cane would accompany him to the dance the day after the holiday morning football game. There wasn't anybody special he planned to bump into that evening but thought it would be nice to encounter somebody who would befriend his enthusiastic personality.

Once again, the outgoing attitude started the emotional snowball effect when he arrived a little too early to the activity run by the Student Government Association. Upon entering into the area that was usually used as a cafeteria, he was greeted by the semi-attractive president who also doubled as one of the cheerleaders. Seeing Eddie and knowing his go getter outlook, she immediately greeted him by name and asked him to do a favor by sitting next to the door to collect the money from the patrons coming to the dance. Without thinking, he agreed and took a seat to wait for the first individual to come into the meeting place for the high school graduates who were now in college.

Eddie spent close to two hours collecting five dollars from each of all the students and giving them a free first drink ticket. Despite not even being a part of the organization, he felt his assistance helped the cheerleader out when there was nobody by the door.

Around 10:30 pm, there was a light rain developing and since there wasn't anyone new to the dance, Eddie found it was time to go home. Most of the graduates only came in for a few minutes while Eddie's classmates gave him a nice 'hello'. A few mentioned that he looked nice, all dressed up, while others just went into the hall to obtain what they paid for when they handed the money over to Eddie.

Watching the now dark room that under normal circumstances housed the cafeteria, everybody danced while talking over juices that were being served by other underclassman members to the governmental organization. As a temporary ball continued to spin, the graduates did their traditional power-play by introducing their high school girlfriends to their new social groups. During all this time, Eddie was pleasant to each person that came through the door, forgetting a test's results that he took a couple days ago.

When the band took their final break, the door started to be deadly cold with only the November wind coming through, making the Thanksgiving evening feel like the autumn classic night that the planners wanted the occasion to be remembered by.

Since Eddie was on one cane trying to go from point A to point B while walking straight, the slippery conditions decided to play a dirty trick by taking away the rubber suction of the tip at the bottom of the wooden apparatus. Down Eddie went, right into the soft but muddy grass. Hoping that no one saw what just happened, he grabbed the cane and did everything he was told at three years of age to do when he fell: climb up the cane until standing.

As he conquered the upright condition, he tried to wipe clean the mud off his pants while wondering if anybody saw what just occurred. Looking around and seeing not a soul, he felt comfortable knowing that the act did not bring any circus-like attention.

Another fun and exciting night, he thought to himself, getting to his car dripping wet.

Despite the Frank Stallone Independent anthem being over for a couple minutes, Eddie could still hear it in his head while watching the Savannah, Georgia news.

"Wow," he said to himself.

"Three teens were killed early tonight while drinking turned deadly when someone thought they had cocaine on them, the partiers never really knew what hit them," the anchor woman said.

It gives new meaning to the words, 'say no to drugs', Eddie thought, putting his head to the pillow.

Dealing With Own Baggage

It seemed as easy as 1–2–3, getting from the gate to baggage claim then arriving on the curbside pick-up with her favorite saddle in hand.

A sweater that seemed necessary back in New Jersey now was a burden, as the North/South International Airport showed off its number one tourist destination promotion. As her Top Siders hung over the ledge to the roadway, she watched as the Southern Dominican Catholic University van came into sight and in a motion reminiscent to kicking her stirrups out she stepped back onto the curb. The driver opened the doors with a Bahamas style smile and a "Welcome to Southern Dominican Catholic University, Danielle Lynne."

And at that moment, it dawned on her that she was home in a new place with the understanding they actually knew her name just like the old lady taking entries at the horse show.

"Well, thank you, it's my saddle; please be careful." At that moment, the driver found humor in the comment, thinking that Eddie was going to have someone to talk to this semester.

"Your saddle, do you have anything else?"

"Hopefully at the post office when I get to campus."

"I am sure it will be, Danielle Lynne, I am sure it will be."

Closing the van door, it was now time for the classrooms that were down the highway and Eddie was only about 530 miles north of their spot.

"So, Danielle Lynne, have you ever ridden a horse on a beach without one of those saddles?" the driver asked, pulling out into the South Florida traffic.

"No, I am a competitor and never have ridden on a beach without one of my saddles."

"You should try it sometime."

"When I have the time but right now I need to do a job."

Continuing to chuckle, the driver smirked, *Yes, we know you have a job to do.*

Meeting of the Minds

Bobbi had her portable color television already out and plugged in, with a soap opera featuring a hospital setting on the screen. She had been watching the series since the candy striper days. Some thought it was the fictional town in the script; however, her mother's persuasion was the actual impact to enter into the nursing profession.

Dressed in a traditional red-and-white volunteer vest, 'daddy's little girl' came home for lunch only to be greeted by her mother in the adult white uniform, and this innocent image over a peanut butter jelly sandwich stuck with the adolescent who went on to study the craft.

"Room 103," could be heard down the hall and Bobbi stood up, followed by looking out the hall to a short black-haired, preppie character flopping around, while a blue bag thing acted like a pocket book.

"Room 103?" she squeaked.

"I am Bobbi Barnes," another voice came out of the Room 103 doorway.

"Daniel Lynne," the one waddling down the corridor answered with one hand outstretched in a friendly gesture.

"Room 103."

Once inside the dorm room, she dropped the blue bag dependent on her shoulder to the ground.

"What is that?" the nursing student asked.

"A saddle."

"A saddle," Bobbi answered, "my friend has one of those; he rides horses."

"Really?" Danielle Lynne replied, amazed that a guy really rode horses.

"He is an equestrian," Bobbi mentioned, "and he is from New Jersey."

"Really?" Danielle Lynne sounded interested, "do you know his name?"

"Eddie," Bobbi answered, "Eddie Patrick."

"Why does that name sound familiar?"

At that moment, Bobbi just broke into an uncontrollable laugh and this just reinforced the fact that she was in another phase where things were going to be different.

"Eddie Patrick is a trip, not literally, yes, literally, look, Danielle Lynne, the one thing that Southern Dominican *Catholic*," Bobbi said, inflecting on the word 'Catholic' like it was stage direction in a theatrical script, "University does is not to take things lying down."

"I assume you are a nursing student."

"Well, it is a dead giveaway like your saddle," she said taking the prop off her hands in the small set that usually was bigger on a stage.

Starting to be more relaxed, she noticed that Bobbi already chosen the bed. It really did not matter since they both looked exactly alike while the spacing really had no bearing on the situation.

"I hope you didn't mind."

"No."

"Well, I have to admit, the Sisters are at it again."

"What do you mean?" Danielle Lynne inquired.

"Pairing things up, Eddie's old friend with his new friend—that was an interesting decision on their part."

There Is Always a Morning After

Around the same time The Great Satan was stepping off onto the grounds of *County Line Stables,* the phone rang in Eddie Patrick's motel room. As he reached over to pick it up and put it to his ear, in a bleary tone, he spoke the word, "Hello."

On the other end, there was nothing more than a buzz, so he placed the receiver back on the cradle and stared at the red lights that represented the clock.

While he was still in a semi-conscious state, his thoughts started to overcome his mind and the past visions which he remembered started to invade his soul like a movie running at the cinema.

Waking up was a tough thing on that Sunday morning with the Thanksgiving holiday nearly completed, and tomorrow it was time to return to reality and school to prepare for something: goals for the future.

Dead silence engulfed the high school student's bedroom, and in the distance, his mother could be heard speaking on the phone. Since it was early in the morning, the only thing what Eddie was able to make out of the conversation was test and scores. Knowing exactly what exam it was, he knew the answer to the gossip that his mother was making to the neighbor. Eddie found out the result on Tuesday and it was Sunday on the holiday weekend. Lying there alone, he could hear laughter and the receiver put on its cradle.

"Eddie, are you up?" he could hear coming down the hall.

"No."

"Eddie, did you hear back on that test you had in school last week?"

"Umm…"

"Mrs.…." Eddie didn't hear the name, "said her son got his back already, how did you do?"

It seemed at that moment Eddie Patrick did not know what to say, but did reflect that it was a good weekend, lonely but a good relaxing couple days.

Once again back in the present, another Savannah, Georgia television reporter was on the screen, talking about a car accident of a bunch of teens that were smoking pot.

"I should have just said no."

Training Temptation

Angel Damien grabbed a hold of The Great Satan and walked him off the trailer, and he just peered around at his new surroundings with new wonderment. Noticing horses in the grassy field, the chestnut mare just let out a whinny that would scare the daylights out of the lay person.

"Angel, just walk him around the show ring a few times then loose in the paddock," Mr. Hawthorne said, walking out of the country-style house on the farm surrounded by modern day life, "Danielle Lynne will be here tomorrow to school her before starting classes, so right now she can relax."

"Who is Danielle Lynne?" the jockey style equestrian asked back, working really hard.

"Our new boarder."

After finishing the lap, Angel Damian took her off the lead line and watched the beautiful animal trot into the area that resembled a garden salad.

"Nice horse," Angel Damian said to herself.

"Yeah, Angel, except for the fact the only one who can ride that pony is Danielle Lynne," Mr. Hawthorne answered the comment.

"Why is that?"

"I do not know but later today I would like Eddie Patrick to try her out."

"Why is that?"

"He may be good for her; he has a very weak leg."

The two looked at each other and smiled, thinking maybe this was exactly what their 'star' needed to recover.

Modern Day Scriptures

With a stack of information in his hands, Peter King stopped by the Chapel that was the centerpiece to Southern Dominican Catholic University. First thing he noted was the sculpture that hung over the place where the magical ceremony took place at least once every day and every hour on the hour on Sundays.

Putting the 'work' in one of the pews, he sat down for a couple minutes and it seemed that what was important a couple minutes ago took a trip to distance itself from reality. As the tranquil water dripped, nothing could be heard, only Peter's thoughts while the half-naked man stripped off his dignity but holding his true values on the two pieces of wood.

Staring down the artistic rendering helped create a magical conversation that only Peter knew what was about in the peaceful exercise. Unlike traditional pictures, the artist did not have Peter kneel down; instead, the director just watched him sit there patiently in deep thought, which on the surface was blank but in reality was very refreshing. As the golden brass on the consecration box gleamed, Peter kept his eyes focused but then all of a sudden decided to get up while gathering his information. There was a noise in the non-meditated world, but Peter really did not pay any attention; instead, he was back into the 'work alcoholic' mode that was debatable if it was in good faith of the statues that lined the building created for sanctuary.

Leaving one of the campus priests, he entered into the main spiritual theater and stepped up onto the stage. Looking at the students with the thought the semester was starting again as another chapter, the religious leader reminded himself will be written with new characters coming while some preparing to end when the season had its finale.

Things Are Starting to Register

"Danielle Lynne," the old lady called from the back of the office, still looking into the computer.

And from the middle of the mass-marketed small college came a pipsqueak sound saying, "That is me."

"Well, Miss Lynne, your total cost came to four thousand, three hundred and sixty-eight cents for the first semester, sophomore year, here at Southern Dominican University," the lady tallied, walking toward the counter where the new student had her arms crossed, leaning on the rectangular table.

"So, my credits from New Jersey went through."

"Yes, they did, just like you took those courses here, welcome to the class of 1988."

"Thank you," Danielle Lynne responded with a unique warm feeling of being welcomed, "and it is Danielle Lynne, I have two first names."

Walking out into the golden sunshine, Danielle Lynne noticed the chapel in front her and the guy coming out of the biblical-looking doors with information in his hands.

At that moment, the powerful sensation took hold in her eyes and suddenly the feeling was short-lived as Bobbi Barnes came very close to her, riding a bicycle.

"Hey, roomy, what's up," the nursing student started the conversation.

"Hi, Bobbi, nothing much, just registering for class on Monday," she explained in the Friday dew, mist-styled morning.

"Ah! Yes, it is our sophomore year. You know they say we think we know everything, but in reality we do not know anything."

"Yeah, this was much different than the community college I took courses at last year."

Peddling in a slow motion, even Bobbi knew she was back in a special place when the Chapel came into view.

"That was the selling point to me for attending Southern Dominican Catholic University," Bobbi retorted, pointing to the building right in front.

"My mom graduated here but this is my first time here," Danielle Lynne honestly continued the conversation, knowing the spiritual aspect affected her too but really did not want to acknowledge the fact.

"So, what are you doing for lunch?"

"I do not know."

"Well, I need to hit the mall, so you want to join me?"

"Yeah, but I need to get everything done today, since tomorrow I need to get back up to the barn to check on The Great Satan."

"The Great Satan?"

Laughing at how it sounded, Danielle Lynne innocently replied, telling her new friend that it was her large pony: the most important thing in her life and this was the reason she chose South Florida's warm climate as the place to continue striving to understand the main reason behind sitting in a classroom.

Thinking about her gesture, she at once agreed. Bobbi started to steer the two wheels to the dorms, while Danielle Lynne took another glance at the steeple and came to the closure—she was home.

Fuel for Thought

With the two canes in each hand, Eddie Patrick made it up the small step, went into the convenience store, and inquired at the desk for assistance to pump the gas at self-served prices. Turning around, he could see two very attractive females, with one wearing a Florida Gators tee-shirt and the other in tight orange shorts.

Gainesville was just a few miles past the Florida State line, which he was ready to pass in the next half-hour. Behind the counter, the attendant talked on his walkie-talkie and all of a sudden someone appeared to assist Eddie with the gasoline.

"Can you fill it with regular?" Eddie said handing a credit card in his parents' name to the employee.

"Sure can," he replied while behind the cash register the card was swiped.

While all this was going on, the girls were having a jolly time giggling their way through the potatoe chip aisle, which Eddie followed them to, putting one cane in front of the other, resembling a four-legged animal.

Eddie could not help but admire the orange on the tan skin when one bent down and those physical energies stimulated him for a few moments.

In reality, he beat them to the cash register as they went back to the refrigerator section to pick up the beer.

Looking a second time at the sign, which stated nineteen not twenty one, related the message back to him why the Gator girls were on the Georgia side of the state line. As his supplies were tightly wrapped in two plastic bags, Eddie proceeded to put the handle on the wrist and navigated through the door in an independent fashion. The two girls did notice the action and while paying for their bag, observed him get into the car displaying New Jersey plates.

"I really like seeing that," one said to the other.

"What is 'that'?" the blonde asked the brunette.

"Total independence."

Pulling out, Eddie took in his rearview mirror and was rewarded with one more second of stimulation and caught the brunette giving one of those collegiate smiles.

Only one more state to go, Eddie thought positively to himself, *and I will be back home at Southern Dominican Catholic University.*

Mind Games

Angel Damien had a feed bucket in hand in the grassy field, trying to lure The Great Satan to a place where she could catch him with the grain temptation. Picking up his head, The Great Satan came right over upon command, making it look like she fell for Angel's gullible scheme.

"That was easy," the thin, waif teenager observed, bringing the pony in to be saddled.

"Just get on him for a few minutes, when Eddie comes, I want him to ride. I think the pair will be good for each other," Mr. Hawthorne announced from the patio that overlooked the schooling ring.

Like a deceptive educator, The Great Satan played the role of doing anything she wanted and patiently gave Angel his one hundred percent attention, watching with a keen eye the saddle go on his back while the bridle fit smoothly in the mouth, giving him something to play with that did not taste like grass.

Amazingly, the chestnut was making Angel Damian's job really easy and when she started toward the mounting block, Mr. Hawthorne waited and watched his assistant trainer work with the new arrival.

"I am going to go out to the big field," Angel Damian exclaimed to her boss.

"You do that, let me know how it goes," Mr. Hawthorne returned the gesture, starting back into the house.

Stirrups formally adjusted and with a scene straight from the back stretch at the race track being the setting, Angel Damian had the 'hot walker feeling' guiding The Great Satan to the grassy field with a few fences. Once inside the natural ring, she broke the horse into a trot and Angel Damian was able to pick up the proper diagonal by rising in her seat when The Great Satan's outside leg went forward.

"Easy," Angel Damian communicated with her partner as things started to get friskier. Mr. Hawthorne could see the action from the kitchen window while cleaning the glasses that once housed the Crystal Drink iced tea that his morning lessons were downing, before leaving to get ready to go back to school.

"Ah, yes, it is still The Great Satan," Mr. Hawthorne snickered, watching the Barn Manager struggle while pulling on the reigns.

Seeming to be confused, Angel Damian brought him back to a walk by sitting calmly into the saddle, which gave The Great Satan the signal to slow down to a walking motion.

Taking a few more steps, Angel Damian caught her breath and decided to see what type of canter there was and once she made her commitment, the wannabe jockey gave a strong kick with the feet that were in the stirrups, expecting a slow transition.

Not liking that motion, The Great Satan became really annoyed and decided to break into the third-level speed without telling the rider.

This took Angel Damian by surprise and it only took a few seconds for that lead outside leg, which was emphasized by the canter to turn into a full outright gallop. This sudden change knocked Angel Damian off balance and this loss to her rhythm made the horse go one way while she went the other. Picking up on this sensation very early, Angel Damian grabbed onto the mane, which quickly slipped out of her hands. Next thing she noticed was a swirling motion and the ground coming toward her, which made her hands forget about the straight, thin hair that lined The Great Satan.

Like a gymnast looking to do a tumble, Angel Damian's strong arms braced the rest of her body as she hit the grassy field. Not being able to stop, The Great Satan continued on at a gallop to the other side of the field and decided to stop for a late morning snack, putting her head down, which in turn brought the reigns ever so close to being off her neck.

Starting to stand up, Angel Damian took a swipe at her pants to clean off the yellow stain but was more concentrated on watching The Great Satan take happy hour before lunch.

"Cheesus," Angel said underneath her breath.

She could hear in the background the words, "Is everything okay?"

Watching The Great Satan intently, Angel Damian blew off the question, hoping the horse was not going to break the leather strap that was over her head.

"Don't you dare," the groom assistant trainer said, staring into the chestnut's eyes like it was a mind war of biblical proportions.

Knowing he got her goat, The Great Satan released the leather hostage by flipping the apparatus back into the right place and trotted back to the mount, who was standing like a jockey ready to go back into the gate.

"All right, you know, I am one of the best catch riders in the state."

The Great Satan just took the comment in while chomping on the bit and watching Angel Damian with a sarcastic grin that turned into a sneeze all over the best catch rider in the state, followed by her using the green polo as a tissue.

Mr. Hawthorne watched the episode from the porch, lighting a pipe, snickering, taking a stroke to his red curly hair, smiling, "This horse will be fine for Eddie Patrick."

Crossing into the Sunshine State

Fiddling with the radio, Eddie Patrick slowed down when he saw the red-and-blue lights on the Ford behind him, watching him speed by and click on the flashers once he passed Eddie's car, leaving the college bound student in the dust. But the sudden explosive excitement reminded the driver about one of the times he saw this type of emergency situation.

Eddie could hear the phone conversation in his ear as he looked into the early morning mirror. Next to the regular toiletries was a razor with the retractable blade that popped out from last night when the date-less Eddie tried to use it to look grown up.

"Eddie, why did you tell me you did not get the test back, Mrs.…," he could hear his mother come down the hall, "said…."

Most of what Eddie heard was jumbled as he looked at the sharp object which lay near the sink. Knowing that it now was going to be an issue, he stared at the silver razor and then at the wrists, wondering if this was a way off the highway and a chance to stop and rest in peace without any more punching bag verbal communication.

As he could hear the strong footsteps come down the hallway, he took the sharp object in his left hand and proceeded to rub it up against the spot where, only a few days earlier, his watch told him the time. Once the skin opened, Eddie watched the red liquid flow out of his skin in a way that seemed like a water fountain spouting water. Holding back the pain, he tried it on his second wrist, and with the same results, the blood started to trickle out like it had been released from prison.

"Eddie, I need to ask you…," Eddie heard as his mind started to feel faint.

While he was doing the speed limit, the mile markers started to wind down and Eddie knew the lower they went, the closer to his destination the car was coming, while soon he was going to be back home. Looking to his right, he saw the flashing light car parked in front of the Gator Girls automobile and laughed, wondering how they were going to get out of this one.

Schooling Round

"Okay, I have this one so the sunlight won't be in my eyes."

"That is fine, I like the window," Danielle Lynne agreed, surveying the room.

Occupying one of the cold wooden desks were three second-year nursing books which intimidated Danielle Lynne for a minute, but she found the other table near the window to be much cleaner, ready for her to make it a study home.

"Here is the situation: I study a lot but mostly at the library where it is open with people," Bobbi announced, taking control of the situation.

"That is fine," Danielle Lynne quietly listened.

"Well, I do have to run. I have to get over to the hospital. There is this young child who almost died yesterday, and I just wanted to make sure he is doing well."

"That is so sweet," Danielle Lynne admired her genuine remark.

Walking out, Bobbi closed the door slowly but Danielle Lynne could hear her new roommate chuckling, saying to one of her sorority sisters, "I told her about the young child at the hospital. She is from the north, right?"

Yeah, I am from the north, Danielle Lynne thought about it, knowing this is exactly what she wanted.

Changing Attitudes

Inside the West Palm Beach Rest Stop, on the turnpike, Eddie Patrick made his way out of the bathroom, now wearing his tan britches and black boots with a serious look, ready to attack the final half-hour to the trip. Carrying his gym bag on his wrist with the white sweat ban, he was getting ready not for the final mile markers, instead the training session. He pulled out of the parking space and in a few minutes the car was back traveling south, only miles from the county line exit featuring a racetrack next to a future football stadium.

As the car slowly made its way to the yield side at the entrance to the turnpike, the two time National Disabled Physically Challenge Handicap Champion individual at the walk reached for a Bruce Springsteen tape to put into his deck beneath the radio. When the static filled Miami radio stations were replaced, Eddie seemed too focused and watched the Davie Florida mile signs come down in number. He was almost there.

Buying an Education

What *is the purpose of college?* Danielle Lynne thought to herself, browsing the bookstore texts. With a credit card in hand, the nationally ranked junior equestrian remembered why she was making these investments in the college level literature when all she really wanted to do was compete.

"These are academic theories built on thought while reality is putting the theories in these books into practice," she mumbled to herself and her roommate was right behind the new resident to the school.

"It is about commitment," Bobbi snuck up behind her, "sort of like marriage, except this one you can get out of and change without being a sinner."

Danielle Lynne just broke into a hysterical laugh, since she had never heard a comparison like that before and it fit her mindset, coming from a community college a year ago.

"So, what you are saying; if you wanted to get out of nursing you can get out without sinning?" Danielle Lynne continued the conversation.

"No, actually, my parents would cut me off if I changed majors," she replied.

"So what do you want to do with all these ten pound literature barbells?" Bobbi inquired.

"Make money," Danielle Lynne said.

"Oh," the future health care worker responded, walking away with one of those blond-haired smirks, "She is from the north."

Following Bobbi down the aisle, Danielle Lynne gave one of those apologetic smiles.

"That is not what I mean, look, sciences are just not my thing, so the only way I could stick around the horses is a degree that makes you think and make money," she said, looking at a 1986 calendar.

"Oh, I meant to tell you I have a friend who loves horses, his name is Eddie Patrick," the future health care worker repeated to make Danielle Lynne think.

That name struck Danielle Lynne in an interesting way, to the point that she put down the flowerily monthly guide, saying, "Why does that name sound familiar?"

Angela's Written Scripture

As the Bruce Juice, which the New York City Dee Jays like to call it, came to the final song on *The River* cassette tape, the white Chevy Nova without air-conditioning came to rest at the farm that housed horses, dogs, and the one monkey which watched all the activity like a parrot looking to take back control.

Eddie grabbed his two canes and popped out of the car where he was met by Mr. Hawthorne.

"Mr. Hawthorne, how are you? That instruction really helped out last year when I went to Nationals," Eddie responded.

"Very good, Eddie, and it is Nate."

"Oh yeah. It's Nate."

"Oh, by the way, how was it at the walk?"

What Nate Hawthorne was talking about was the disabled horse show that invited cerebral palsy riders to compete against other handicapped or disabled people. Or maybe that was physically challenged athletes. Funny they never disputed the medical papers in Eddie's file when it said cerebral palsy, but the northerners never knew what to make of the person who listed the name 'Saint' as a middle name.

"Well, Eddie, yesterday we got a shipment of horses and there is one that I would like you to try out."

"He is called The Great Satan," Angel interrupted, still brushing off her pants.

"The horse is called The Great Satan," Eddie sounded enthusiastic, "what, did Linda Blair like use to own and show her?"

"No," Mr. Hawthorne said in a chuckling, disappointed tone and then made up a story, "instead, a junior rider named Amber Newman used to show her before giving the sport up but that was all they told me."

Shuffling down the embankment through the stone, an observer could see the cerebral palsy word but once stopped despite the bent knees, it was hard to see any conflicts except the white sweat bands on the wrists.

"Mr. Hawthorne, The Great Satan is all ready to be tacked up and in the stall, and the step stool you asked for is in the tack room," Angel announced to her boss, "I will just be up at the main house."

"Sure, Angel, thanks," Nate said halfway down to the red stable which was basically, in the western tradition, without any fancy indoor rings. Instead, the stalls ran up to the ring, leaving room for a walkway and places to saddle horses.

Once Eddie stepped on the cement entry, he saw the chestnut that looked him straight in the eye and bowed his head to scratch the leg.

"Great Satan, how are you?" Eddie said, hearing the equestrian tack jingle as the horse popped up his head.

Mr. Hawthorne dragged the horse out of the stall and The Great Satan, noticing the canes, did not take off the stare on his other four-legged friend.

By the time the stool was in place, Angel Damian was back from her trip to the house and assisted Nate by holding the horse's head as Eddie, now wearing a black velvet helmet, climbed the two-step stool and once on top, he placed one foot in the stirrup while the trainer assisted in moving the left leg to the other side.

Knowing he had a rider on his back, The Great Satan now stood at attention with Angel Damian letting go and walking away.

"Oh, by the way, there were no papers, Eddie," Angel Damian said.

"What did she mean by that?" Eddie looked down at Mr. Hawthorne who just shrugged his shoulders with the response.

"Sort of like your medical file or how things were handled back then."

"Walk on, Great Satan," Eddie commanded.

A Sign Meant

"Oh, Peter," Bobbi could be heard down the hall as she made her way down the dark pathway that was known as the Communication School, "I know you're in there, Peter; I see the light on."

"Go away, no one is home," As she heard the nursing student in her second year of college come closer, she scampered out into the hallway which had a dim tinge to it like an artistic design in a preppie horror movie.

"Bobbi, Bobbi Barnes, how good is it to see you."

"Peter, Peter King, I need a favor from you."

"Anything for the nursing school," he said, holding the door for the lady.

"New recruits," she said.

"New recruits?"

Now in the well-lit office, Bobbi took it upon herself to flip through the black-and-white photos that were lying on the desk.

"Yeah, we have some freshman class coming in this year and our Dean wants something in the paper."

"Oh, she does," Peter went into his editor mode while Bobbi put her arm around him in a friendly way.

"Oh, she does, sure, Bobbi, anything for you," he finished his sentence.

"Thank you, Peter."

"Weren't you a freshman last May?"

"Yeah, and now I know everything, 3:15, Monday afternoon, all right."

"Sure, my camera will be filled with film and I will find space in the paper."

"Well, you can add another page and then you can fill more advertising." Bobbi suggested while opening the door.

"3:15, Monday afternoon."

Testing Temptation

Finally without his canes for about an hour or so, Eddie Patrick walked the chestnut pony without any known documented past in a way that was athletically strong. It felt very comfortable and immediately, the two looked very attractive as a pair despite the sometime spastic motion that could plague the rider at times.

"You look good up there," the trainer on the ground watched and observed with the comment.

"Yeah, very nice," Angel Damian repeated, knowing that Eddie Patrick had something different that she did not have when aboard the prince-like mount.

"She feels nice," Eddie remarked, bringing the reigns to the proper place.

Already, the two made a full circle around the ring while the rail birds claiming to have knowledge concentrated on the work that was being performed.

"When you get to the next tree I want you to trot," Mr. Hawthorne requested.

Right then and there, Eddie focused in on the Arbor object lying at the ring's next bend. Collecting the leather straps in front of him called reigns, he held a firm in control grip which made The Great Satan feel like he was ready to do some work on the late August afternoon.

"Trot, Great Satan," the two on the ground heard when the pair passed the trunk.

Mr. Hawthorne concentrated on Eddie's leg as it did not move an inch unlike regular riders who would have the natural instinct to kick. Using basic voice commands and motions controlled by the reigns, The Great Satan understood everything that was asked during the session that lasted about an hour.

Eddie repeated everything during the final thirty minutes and upon leaving the circular dirt arena, he glanced at the jump that was set up for one of the riders who was trying to earn points for the Junior Championships in New York City.

"Good ride, Eddie, good ride," Mr. Hawthorne stated while Angel Damian came by with a towel.

"Good boy," she said, wiping the gookety gook out of his nose, "good boy."

"Horse belongs to my niece, she should be here tomorrow or the next day depending when she is finished registering at school," Mr. Hawthorne said, leaving out on purpose that they were living on the same campus. He figured destiny should take its proper course and his comments went through Eddie like water that he desperately needed in the summer South Florida heat.

Getting to Know the Ring

Scampering down the stairs, Peter King pulled out his cash card as he passed by the post office. Standing there next to the boxes was a cute, little brown-headed preppie girl searching for the proper number to put her key into the lock.

"Well, hello, and what is your name?" the reporter asked.

"Danielle, Danielle Lynne."

"And where are you from?"

"New Jersey."

"And what is your major?"

"A degree," she responded, "one that will make me think."

"I am Peter King," he said, putting out a greeting hand, "and I am from here in South Florida."

"What is your major?" she asked in a shy way.

"Communication Arts, I run the paper upstairs," Peter continued with the questions, "I have a friend from New Jersey who should be here tonight."

"Let me guess, Eddie Patrick."

"How did you know?"

"I am roommates with Bobbi Barnes."

"Really, you are," Peter started to remark, "friends?"

"Oh," Danielle Lynne replied.

"Well, I have to get some money out of the bank but I will probably see you later."

Walking away, Danielle Lynne thought what an interesting set of questions he had asked, *What's your name, where are you from and what's your major?* Looking back, she noted in her mind that he forgot one, *What year are you?*

That one I will keep for myself, she pondered, knowing she must keep up with the course, being sure all her memorization academic strides were handled smoothly.

Balancing Act

"So, you probably want off The Great Satan," Angel Damian wanted to know before heading back up to the house to end the day.

"Let me walk one more time around the ring and then he will be cooled down," Eddie answered.

With loose reigns and allowing The Great Satan to have his head Danielle Lynne's prized chestnut plodded outside the simple ring that had one wooden board that defied the schooling area.

When Eddie reached the furthest point, The Great Satan stumbled, creating a feeling that caught Eddie in a way that was very strange. He tried so hard to catch his balance but that simple skill was missing from his brain. Next thing Eddie knew, he was slowly slipping to the ground, Angel Damian caught the action from the corner of her eye as did Mr. Hawthorne.

It was like watching a slow motion video as Eddie simply slipped to the ground and threw out his hands to block his fall. Making sure The Great Satan was out of the way, he side-stepped the action and watched him fall gracefully. Angel was the first one on the scene, carrying the step stool while Mr. Hawthorne monitored the situation from the patio table sitting, smoking his pipe in a very relaxed setting.

"I was kidding," Angel Damian tried to reassure Eddie, helping him stand while The Great Satan just stood there watching the two, "you have a decision, your canes are over there and we are here."

"I will ride him back to the stalls."

Angel, who designed a way for Eddie to get mounted on the horse aided with a step ladder at her side put into play the plan to fix the problem. This simple task easily assisted not helped Eddie back onto The Great Satan. It only took a few minutes for Eddie to dismount in the traditional sense when the pair arrived at the stable. Angel handed him his canes, noticing the swollen lip that now was a fixture like makeup on a horror movie character.

Taking the bridle off and then replacing it with the halter, followed by hooking a lead line, The Great Satan was guided out to the grassy pasture by his groom. Before letting him go feed on the salad that was in the field, Angel grabbed a brush and rubbed the dark markings created by sweat.

Her next move was to allow The Great Satan to have that South Florida natural salad, but once he had his freedom, the horse turned himself over for a grassy back rub to end the day.

"Oh, boy, you are a trip," she said, seeing Mr. Hawthorne having a chat with Eddie before he headed home for dinner.

Walking the Course

Taking a walk around the square like mall area, Danielle Lynne enjoyed the fresh air as she got used to the campus. They say, "If you take a cruise ship, the first thing you do is explore the boat," and that was what she was doing, checking out her new home from top to bottom. Granted it was not that big but just like an indoor arena the size did not have anything to do with the challenges that lay ahead starting first thing in the morning.

It took her about ninety minutes to find the different classrooms she would be attending, and she planned how she was going to get to them in the amount of time allowed by the judges which in the sense would be the alarm clock or the professor running this important thing that now engulfed her life.

Walking up the steps, she saw a car pull into the handicap space and a cute guy stepped out in tan riding pants.

She was now ready for the course.

Coming in Two Terms

A romantic warm sunset engulfed Southern Dominican Catholic University when Eddie and his fat lip pulled into the space the school gave him at the start of his freshman year.

"Eddie, you finally arrived," Peter could be heard off in the distance with a camera strap around his shoulder.

Now that the car was stopped and while emptying the fully packed automobile, Eddie knew his good friend was primed for getting him out of another independent challenge.

"Sure, you probably need help, oh, sorry, assistance to unpack the car," Peter said.

It was very interesting how fast an able-bodied person could unpack a car bound for college when their two hands are totally free, but Eddie needed physical support with the canes since his brain did not allow the balancing act to occur when standing unassisted by any aides.

As Eddie waited in this dorm room, which was open and totally clean, his friend brought all the stuff inside then dropped it on the bed that did not have any sheets.

"Welcome back!" Peter said as the luggage entered into the square room which had a size that could fit the bed and desk with not much room to spare.

"Thanks so much, I am going to have to get unpacked here," he said.

"Well, later, Truman Johnson. I know the baseball team was going to join us for a trip down to Denny's if you wanted to join us?" his friend let him know, looking at the stuff on the bed, "be honest, Eddie, it is just going to be there in the end anyway."

"First off, I have to take care of this busted lip."

"Yeah, what happened, herpes back in Jersey?"

"No, I slipped off this new horse."

"Yeah, I know. Bobbi is on call tonight so you may want to go over and see her and put some ice on that wound."

"Come back around 9:30?" Eddie questioned.

"Yeah, sure," Peter said with a cautious tone.

Documentation of a Nutcase or Educator

"Mr. Hawthorne," Angel Damian said while putting the final dish into the washer then turning it on.

"Yes, Angel."

"I know it is not my place but…"

"Yes, oh, by the way, great steak you cooked."

"All right, it is not my place but The Great Satan has no papers and to put Eddie on with all these unknown factors is a big chance."

"I know and it is also my niece's horse."

"Well, that too. How is she going to fit college in with a rigorous show-jumping training schedule?"

Mr. Hawthorne placed the pipe in his hands and smiled, "Structure, Angel, structure."

"How do you get everything accomplished every day?"

"Structure."

"Yes, Angel, structure, without the horses Danielle Lynne would not have any structure and just wallow away without a clue about the division between fantasy and reality."

"And is there something wrong with that?"

"No structure."

"The horse is a nutcase and he has no papers, let alone structure."

Mr. Hawthorne just retired to his chair in the middle of the living room with the pipe in his hand, thinking to himself that it was going to be an interesting fall; structurally speaking.

Going for First-Aid

One blue bedsheet lay across the mattress as Eddie Patrick put a key in the hole to lock the door. There was hustling and bustling throughout the dorm while other students seemed to get settled. Still wearing dirtied-up riding pants and a white polo shirt, Eddie made his way down into the reception hall that had the entrance to the pool courtyard. Across the relaxing area was one of the girls' living quarters and on the first floor Bobbi Barnes' room was the acting 24-hour nursing station.

It only took a few minutes for the college student with two canes to make across the squared-off area occupied by sun worshippers during the day. When he came to the double door, the canes went into one hand, like everybody told him to do it, and one hand reached for the door which opened with ease. Using the rubber stopper, the cane kept the green obstacle from closing as he walked in the hall. Once inside, the equestrian went to the guest check in and asked for Bobbi Barnes. She was in and came out into the hall wearing sweatshirt and shorts in bare feet.

"Well, welcome back to South Florida, Eddie Patrick," she started, "what can I do for you? Oh."

"I need an ice pack."

"Come on in, that thing looks yucky," Bobbi said while grabbing the visitors' pass.

Eddie followed the nursing student down the hall, enjoying his time inside forbidden territory.

Bobbi's room was dimly lit and looked very comfortable, unlike Eddie's 'let's get by and the mattress is there to sleep on' attitude.

"So, what happened?"

"Slipped off a horse and hit a fence post."

"Ohh…kay"

Danielle Lynne was on the pay phone inside when the four-legged guy wearing riding pants entered into the scene. After the conversation with Uncle Nate was done, she made her way down the hallway back to the room she had with Bobbi. And at that moment it clicked that Eddie was getting some nursing attention. By the time Danielle Lynne entered into the dorm room, the ice packs were broken and Eddie was applying the cold feeling to his lip.

"Horse knocked him off," she said to Danielle Lynne upon her entrance.

"Hi," was her shy response.

"This is Eddie Patrick." Bobbi was being a caregiver by introducing Danielle Lynne to the mildly wounded fellow student.

"Hi, Eddie," Danielle Lynne repeated.

Setting Up for a Double Play

Truman Johnson flipped his key chain in the air as he walked down the dark path that led to the main social hall where the newspaper office was located on the second floor. While the keys were in the air, he opened the door then caught the chain in the same motion, keeping his foot from allowing the entrance to be blocked. Since the hall was basically empty, only a limited number of lights were needed as the baseball player made his way up the staircase to the journalistic hangout.

"Peter," could be heard.

"I am not here," Peter retorted.

In the night's silence, the keys' jingling could be heard and the stillness broke when Truman came through the door.

"I said I wasn't here but that's all right," Peter said in a comical but serious fashion.

"Hey, how was your summer?" the small school second baseman stated, knowing all he did was work a construction job.

"It was all right," Peter said, still behind a typewriter, banging out on his style key.

"We are going to have a good season this year," Truman remarked, shuffling through the baseball photographs taken last semester, "you coming out for fall practice on Saturday."

"Yeah, I probably can get some shots," Peter agreed.

"Saturday at 3:15 PM is the inter squad game."

"Oh yeah, I can make it," Peter confirmed, finishing writing the final sentence to the story about the diamond team, "are you ready to go?"

"Sure."

"Eddie is coming with us, if you do not mind."

"No, I really do not mind," Truman said, opening the door for Peter.

Tender, Loving Care

As the two dropped their stare at each other and Danielle Lynne returned to her dimly lit desk, Bobbi broke the romantic tension between the two with the crackling of the ice pack.

"Here, Eddie, take this and apply it to your lip every fifteen seconds then rest for five," Bobbi instructed and her northerner friend accepted the suggestion thinking it was pretty structured for just an ice pack.

Putting the canes in the same hands, he pressed the bruise for the prescribed time when Danielle Lynne looked up from the orientation schedule.

"So, what did happen?" she paused "If you do not mind me asking?"

At this point, Bobbi started to roll her eyes, waiting for the horse blah blah blah and Eddie fulfilled her prophecy by telling her the truth.

"I slipped off a horse and hit my lip on the fence post."

"Ow, what horse would have done that???" Danielle Lynne yelped in a petrified voice, knowing no horse would, in its right mind, ever allow something like this to happen.

"His name was The Great Satan," Eddie unknowingly responded.

"I have a horse named The Great Satan," Danielle Lynne really perked up with her glassy eyes open like it was Christmas morning.

"Yes, a chestnut."

At this point, Bobbi had retired to her bed not really knowing what they were talking about, Great Satans and chestnuts. To her, it sounded like Christmas Eve at Linda Blair's house, but she fulfilled her professional duties while returning to her studies despite class not even starting until the morning.

Nose in the print, Bobbi snickered as her new roommates could not take their eyes off each other, and it dawned on Bobbi that this would probably not be that bad of a thing for Eddie. And he looked cute, ready to blush.

"Hey, Danielle Lynne, we are going to Denny's; do you want to come?"

"I have orientation first thing in the morning so I can't but I will see you tomorrow, right?"

Leaving the room, Eddie turned and for the first time in a long while had a comfortable sensation throughout his body.

"Yeah, you will," he was the one with the affirmative statement.

As the door started to close, Danielle Lynne knew the pillow was her next destination; climbing into the bed, she rested on the mattress, all dressed up in sheets.

And looking up to the ceiling, a thought just hit her now that Eddie was already out past the security check point.

"Hey, wait a second, I own The Great Satan and he has already been on him. I have to call Uncle Nate in the morning," she said, looking at the white plaster.

"You have to get to orientation."

"That too."

Going With the Flow

Eddie Patrick sat in his chair in the classroom whose door exited straight to the outdoors, noticing the pickup truck with the logo N/S County Line Stables and wondering if Nathaniel Hawthorne was off to pick up another student to teach them the ways of the world.

Snapping the ball point pen, the professor continued to talk about Herman Hesse's classic observations entitled Siddhartha, which are deemed important and should be tested at the end of the semester to determine what letter goes in the computer in the office where the student drops off the checks. Oh, what an interesting concept about flowing with things, and it reminded Eddie about the true strategy in dealing with the conflict that God gave him to put up with as a protagonist. Just move with the situation. Earlier in the class, which was supposed to end in a few minutes, the PhD instructor asked a question which the C student in high school answered correctly. Despite being a sophomore and supposed to know everything, Eddie found himself proud to come up with the right answer in a college class. It was just like getting the confidence back that he once had in grammar school. Checking his watch, the professor decided to close his lecture on the ancient scripture, which was the cue for everybody to pick up their texts and move on to the next commitment on the day's schedule.

For Eddie, this meant lunch followed by a trip to the library, continuing with dinner in the cafeteria and ending back in the library.

Walking out with two canes in hand, Eddie saw Abigail standing with scotch tape and the poster board stating the message 'The Southern Dominican Catholic University Serpents will be holding a cheerleading tryout next week.'

"Hey, Muffy," Eddie said, now wearing a sports jacket and scarf.

"Oh, Hello, Mister Patrick, Mister Saint Patrick, and it is Abigail," she said, standing up in her outfit which Eddie noticed with a smile despite the heat. It was Eddie's belief that his fashion statement overpowered the situation by presenting a professional appearance which should get noticed.

"So, you never told me; did you enjoy homecoming last year?"

"You were a wonderful escort, thank you."

"How is your fighting Irish boyfriend? Still trying to make the baseball team?"

"Yes," Abigail replied, seeing Eddie's angelic smile.

Abigail, whom Eddie loved to call Muffy, was bailed out by her sorority little brother when her boyfriend was caught in a snow blizzard and was not able to take her as a freshman to the Homecoming dance where she was odds on favorite to be queen.

While coming back from the barn on a Friday night, he saw her crying sitting outside on the dorm room steps wearing her Sorority tee-shirt when Eddie approached her and, following the Greek rules, asked what was wrong. She told her little brother the story and once again organizational protocol stepped in to force Eddie to ask if it would be all right for him to escort her to the Homecoming dance.

Having to change his plans to get a tuxedo, Eddie did not make it to Equestrian practice on that Saturday morning; instead, the local formal rental store was the destination for the weekend. Abigail wearing a strapless dress, Eddie donning both his tuxedo that was haunted by the sporting sweatbands the two attended the event, had their pictures taken and placed as memorabilia into the Delta scrap book.

"Oh, by the way, Ed dee," Abigail came back toward him, tugging at the necklace she was wearing with an 'A,' "This was given to me by the baseball player and it stands for Abigail, not Muffy."

"Oh, sorry, Muffy, if I remember correctly the 'A' in this type of situation."

"Shut up, you're lucky you're cute or I would take your canes away."

Turning her back in a sarcastic motion, Eddie felt really good for a moment, knowing the other Homecoming dances in his life were far behind him in the past.

Schooling over a Fence

Gloves on and with a very delicate feel, Danielle Lynne kept focused on the fence that was in the corner of her eye. There it was when the horse below her went into the ring's deep portion. The red spot in the middle of the fence commanded a stare when the inside hand gently gave a tug, signaling The Great Satan to make a turn to the obstacle that was now straight down the line. Only a second ago, the spot was in the corner of Danielle Lynne's eye, but as she made the turn she kept stalking that mark by turning her head straight ahead while The Great Satan continued giving his rider a rocking chair effect. Going through a final check list made Danielle Lynne prepared to make the simple jump that was used to school. Feeling her seat go back, the straight look combined with the heels down created a look that she was in total control with the obstacle coming closer, and like a trained animal her hands naturally grabbed onto The Great Satan's whitish mane and leaned forward without taking any concentration off the red spot.

Uncle Nate stood there at the ring watching very closely, and the pair engaged the three-and-half foot challenge.

"Nice try, Danielle Lynne," he said from the peanut gallery when the horse went airborne for a second.

Not hearing anything, Danielle Lynne knew she hit the mark perfectly when The Great Satan front hoofs came to rest on the dusty ring bottom.

"Sweet," she could be heard saying underneath her breath when the back legs came back to earth.

"Very nice," the peanut gallery spread the positive reinforcement, "very nice."

Coming out of the three point stance or jumping position, Danielle Lynne returned to having a straight back.

"Danielle."

"Yeah."

"I would like you and Eddie to do the local schooling show together with The Great Satan on Sunday, you do the over fence classes while Eddie will do the flat."

"I really am not interested in the championships of those classes and it will be fun to do it with Eddie."

"Really, Danielle, you are not at all concerned about wasting time?"

"No, it will be fun, it will be something special."

When Danielle Lynne walked The Great Satan out of the ring, the trainer knew his niece had finally found comfort down here in the sunshine state.

Supporting a Figure

Out of her cheerleading outfit and into her boyfriend's Notre Dame Baseball jersey, Abigail strolled outside the elevator door onto the fourth floor where Eddie was laying on the couch asleep.

"Oh, little brother, I need a favor from you," she stated, looking over the side of the couch with the 'A' necklace above Eddie's face.

"It is nice to see you awake and everything."

"Just really tired."

"I said I need a favor."

"What?"

He sat up, and Abigail joined him by sitting on the couch.

"We need some publicity from the tryouts; do you think you can write something up?"

"Write something up?"

Not knowing what she was saying, she affirmed that statement.

"You mean come out, observe the event, and make sure it is all right for all the collegiate community."

"What have you become; Joe Journalism?"

Eddie just looked at her and she peered back.

"It is the cheerleading tryouts, girls in tight leotards, jumping up and down."

Nose to nose, the two felt like something needed to be said.

"As I said, we have the right to come in and objectivity report back to the rest of the community that everything is all right with your club."

"Okay, little brother, I should take that as a yes," the sister to the only sorority at Southern Dominican Catholic University concluded.

Walking away, Eddie watched the athletic strut leave the library, commenting out loud, "Muffy, of course I am going to do a write up."

Turning around, she smiled, "Score one for Abigail." And the Communication Arts student returned to the 'text' he was deeply reading: *How to Catch Someone's Attention with Your Message.*

Exercise Girls

Angel Damian met Danielle Lynne outside the tack room as the top rider took the silver cup and drew some water out of the water bottle.

"God, it gets hot out here," she told the barn manager.

"Excuse me, Danielle Lynne," the barn manager requested when she passed through the small doorway, carrying one of the many saddles that lined the organized storage area.

"Where the…" she paused, "Are the saddle pads?" and Danielle Lynne looked up from the silver chalice, noticing the outburst increased the tension level.

"I thought I saw them."

"Oh, here they are."

"Umm, your horse; do you want him in or out tonight?"

"In," Danielle Lynne replied, putting the tin cup down.

"He has been good despite that ugly noise he makes when others are around him."

"Well, he is a little snotty, that is why I call him The Great Satan, that and…,"

"The fact is there are no papers and he came out of nowhere."

"Five years ago, when I was doing juniors, he came in a shipment and we started to collect points to get to the Nationals, almost made it to the garden, except for that one tricky fence during the *Tri State Regional*."

"Still, he has no papers and I am not too crazy about that."

"But my Uncle Nate…,"

"Yeah, yeah, I know your Uncle Nate."

Angel Damian stepped outside when Danielle Lynne picked up the schooling show entry form and put it into her pocket to take back to school. While leaving the barn for the car, the barn manager caught the rider's eye when she corralled the horse after the quick grassy cocktail.

"Honey, your owner wants you in, happy hour is over."

By the time The Great Satan was tucked into bed, Danielle Lynne had the keys and was waiting for Uncle Nate to give her a ride back to school.

Listening Before Acting

Just like Eddie Patrick was doing across the campus in another building, Bobbi Barnes listened intently to the professor lecture the class about things that had big words. It was interesting to a point as the three hour monologue was coming to a close. But once the clock struck the top of the hour she would not have to deal with it for another week. Granted there was not really any weekly homework assignment except for the 'project' due date and this was a control variable not a test instead, something you had to keep on top of throughout the semester. Furthermore, in this class there wasn't going to be any cramming since the long term assignment was pass or fail. On the first day, it was noted on the syllabus that if you showed up every day, did the routine, and listened in class there should be no problem with the final outcome.

But, there was a stipulation that some in the audience who carefully watched the stage show would, of course, not have a happy ending.

Looking around at her peers, she could pick out a half a dozen or so ready to drop out and change majors, so this sophomore test could be an easy one to ace.

"And to conclude," was heard from the figure with a stage acting presence Bobbi started to close her books and gather her belongings, knowing that another session was done.

Strolling out of the room, the candy bar was the first thing she saw and pulling some change out, she was able to pop in some quick energy in the form of a chocolate bar.

"I guess it is on to another patient," she referenced the next class.

Show Class

As the water came out of the faucet, Mr. Hawthorne stood there cleaning his own dishes from the pony clubbers who came straight from school and needed a snack. Parents told him he had the best iced tea and beat out the 4 H leader hands down. Not having any children of his own due to never getting married, he enjoyed the boisterous commotion every week day when the kids came over to be with the horses. Through the years, he watched them grow up and he made sure they took their studies seriously and applied to colleges. Horses were not really a competition; instead, Mr. Hawthorne believed the activity was an educational experience that complemented the books they read in the classroom.

Oh, by the way, Mr. Hawthorne's students did very well at the area horse shows and on occasion they made it to the National Championship regional finals. But reality has it that around June somebody comes back to tell him they now had a degree in something. Yet, this knowledge has kept him single through the years since there really wasn't anything out there which would lure him away from his scheduled lifestyle.

"All the horses are in," the voice in the darkness announced.

"Thank you, Angel or was that Damian," Mr. Hawthorne quietly whispered, turning off the faucet, grabbing onto the towel right in front of him. "Angel, how is it going with The Great Satan?"

"You know she does not have any papers?"

"I did not ask you that. I was wondering my niece's horse has been here nearly forty eight hours, how he is doing?"

"He is doing fine, I guess," Angel shrugged off the question, coming closer to the counter where a pitcher of Crystal Light was there ready to be poured. While inserting spout into cup, Mr. Hawthorne interjected the question one more time, and the barn manager put the half full glass into the sink while it was still half empty.

"Look, the horse you claim that is so great is a maniac, makes weird noises around the others and you know Eddie fell off him already yesterday."

"Do you want to work here?" Mr. Hawthorne honestly asked.

"Well, a few of the racetracks were looking at me as an exercise rider. I would work mornings then come over here during the afternoon," she replied.

Trying to be as tactful as possible despite the sensitive subject manner, Mr. Hawthorne closed his eyes and quietly said, "Yes, I can do the stalls and chores in the morning, but I really cannot have a backstretch exercise rider around my equestrians, it just would not be right. One, the stress and constant fatigue not only will break you down but the tension would be unbearable on the kids. They are here to learn in the proper environment."

Taking the hint, Angel pulled herself from leaning on the counter by pulling away.

"Learn! What happened? Did one of those rich little snots say something about me quitting school?"

"No, the little rich snots who are prepared every day and have goals did not say anything about burning the desk and getting kicked out of school."

"I guess the racetrack is the best place for me."

"It probably is," Mr. Hawthorne said, softly watching one of his best workers deal with reality.

Not saying another word, she let the door naturally come back and shut while Mr. Hawthorne retorted, "I will send you last week's check once again—sorry, I forgot—and this week's check is in the mail."

In a silent, audible voice he heard a thank you in the darkness.

Boy, did he hate to do that to one of his best workers but the two classes just were not coming together. And the parents had concerns about the element around the barn. Not that it was not fair but it was the truth.

Sitting in her used American-built Ford, she turned on the engine and Jethro Toll came on the speakers. She could still see the silhouette standing there very stern.

"Thank you, Mr. Hawthorne, I learned a lot," putting the car in reverse, trying not to cry but making the promise that she would come back just like the others, successful at something.

An Omen of What's to Come

Eddie was finishing the last of the three miniature glasses that contained a soft drink when Danielle Lynne came up the winding staircase into the area where they fed the students. Handing the card over to the person checking IDs, Danielle Lynne still noticed the door still open, meaning food was still being served. Quickly, she hustled her way across the slick floor in her muckers and made right inside the food server area just in time. Eddie watched intently as the tight riding pants cruised into the area where they were passing out the gourmet cooking that had the appearance of mass marketed meals.

A few seconds later, Eddie continued to observe the slender body come out all dirty and dusty while going through a check list of things to do that evening. Coming to the conclusion that there really wasn't anything pressing, he sat back and let the scene unfold, hoping that this was the start to a romantic comedy and not a slasher film.

"Hi, Eddie, do you mind if I join you?" her timid voice seemed very sweet.

"Sure, Danielle Lynne, no problem."

"Were you at the stable today?"

"Schooling The Great Satan."

"I rode him the other day."

Seated in the chair, Danielle Lynne forgot about the two canes and wondered what he meant by saying he was on her horse the other day. In fact, it dawned on her about the weakness in his legs and how she always had problems as a very young rider when the crop was too big for her hand. It was only a couple years later as a young child visiting friends in Washington D.C that The Great

Satan possessed her riding life at a horse show overlooking the Potomac.

They needed a replacement mount during a pony club rally and the Georgetown University Hospital Benefit Horse Show when, all of a sudden, a young chestnut came into being when two local merchants who bought a booth in the trade show barded the horse for a box of M&Ms which the kids were selling for a dollar. Apparently, no one could stay on the gift horse since the youngsters all kicked too hard while pulling really hard on his mouth. Instead, a frustrated Danielle Lynne was always having a hard time getting the ponies kick-started, so it was two kind men that saw the tears and steered The Great Satan toward to the child who wiped away her tears. Putting the magical saddle on was an enchanting experience and soon, Danielle Lynne was starting to win children's classes then had the gall to take on the adults.

Sitting at the in gate were the two men who just smiled and with a serious yet innocent devilish grin, Danielle Lynne mouthed the word, "Thank you."

One being a man named Calfee and the other carrying the name Straw, both said "You're welcome."

Of course, Danielle Lynne said to herself, feeling a life's challenge coming on, *Of course you got on The Great Satan.*

As they sat there in a friendly way, the conversation throughout covered many topics reflecting around the school year that had just begun and while the talking lasted, Danielle Lynne was relieved to have somebody to converse since sitting up in the wide open space would only make her eat then run.

When everything was finished, she offered to take his dirty plates and Eddie agreed, handing them over, knowing the semester was at the point where the "Hi, what is your name and major," was turning into a little bit more in-depth communication.

Studying the Course

Only one lamp lit the room as Danielle Lynne sat at the wooden desk, reading a text book that was filled with words not related to horses but still had interest enough to write on a legal pad paper. Using a pen, she took notes in this academic hacking exercise and took her glasses off to close her eyes when the door opened. Bobbi stood there in her uniform that represented a ghost.

"Do you know what it is like to have three three-hour classes in the same day?" Bobbi said, walking to her bed.

Looking up from the book, she watched a future nurse just collapse, chuckling, thinking she used to do the same action on a Sunday night after returning from a weekend-rated horse show.

"At least I do not have to do that until next week," Bobbi explained to her pillow with Danielle Lynne hearing every word.

"Why did you take 3 three-hour classes on one day?"

"So I could spend more time on the floors," Bobbi answered the pillow.

"Well, that is enough for tonight," Danielle Lynne replied, turning off the light.

The two girls just laid in silence and if a pin dropped, the disturbance would be heard throughout the room.

"Did you set the alarm?" Bobbi broke the deafening silence.

"I have it for 5:30 am, have to get to the barn."

"That is good, I have an eight o'clock call at the hospital."

"Well, I will be back in the early afternoon and have classes all evening long."

In unison, the two fell asleep, knowing in the next few hours they start the whole day over again.

Being a Barn

"Do you need a leader and side walker, two-time national champion at the walk," Eddie heard during a Saturday afternoon lesson, which he always wanted to experience but, back in New Jersey, never had the confidence or credibility to express what he really wanted out of the sport with exhibitors.

While Danielle Lynne stood there looking like the experienced junior rider that competed constantly in the Northeast, things started to feel special unlike the past where everything was just there and all he was doing was going through the motions, coming back to a walk from the trot where the weak leg equestrian was totally off his diagonal.

Oh, boy, was that bad, he thought to himself, collecting the reigns and taking control of the situation as The Great Satan coughed in a way that seemed like it was his way of getting him back to a friendly manner.

Emerging from the tack room, Danielle Lynne, who was wiping the gookety gook better known as saddle soap off her hands, said, "Two-time National Champion, wow, at this walk at that," she chimed in toward her fellow classmate from a different major.

"He was a gold medalist with a leader but no side walker," Mr. Hawthorne told his niece.

Remembering back to the photo in the magazine she read on the plane along with the newspaper article that caught her eye after a bad date with her then boyfriend, Danielle Lynne headed back into the tack room to put the dried saddle back on the rack. Her uncle, at that point, entered into the dusty ring and stood in the middle, staring, noticing that Eddie was comfortably walking. Since moving with the two seemed to be a natural pair, the trainer decided to shoot some dice and give Eddie Patrick a pop quiz of sorts.

"Eddie, I want you to take the reins and hold them tightly," Mr. Hawthorne administered the question, "when you feel comfortable, pull the outside reign and cluck while saying 'canter'."

Caught off guard but not wanting to make a scene, Eddie did as he was told despite his legs feeling a little uneasy about the transition. He had cantered in the past, but it was by accident and the only reason he did not fall off was due to his quick thinking combined with being able to miraculously lean back in the saddle in an instant.

Securing himself in the stirrups, Eddie pulled on the right reign while clucking a few times. In a dream-like fashion, The Great Satan knew what was going on by responding to the cue that was given to him in a clear, concise manner. For the equestrian who mastered the walk for glory, it was like being in a rocking chair as the transition into a third gait was achieved and Eddie was able to work certain muscles in this relaxed atmosphere.

"Easy," Mr. Hawthorne guided in a smooth voice. "Sit back and enjoy the comfort."

That is what Eddie did aboard the red, brick-colored large pony; he showed off his physical talents like a beauty pageant contestant saying 'look' while strutting the runway. Peering out the door, Danielle Lynne monitored everything from the sidelines and made a final confirmation to take The Great Satan to the schooling competition on Sunday. Since it was an exhibition on the same grounds of a preseason scrimmage, she thought it would be neat to put the national champion in a class that judges the flat work while she plays with her mount over the fences.

Eddie came back to a walk and the coach figure told Eddie to cool down by walking outside the ring and praised him with a job well done.

"They looked like a perfect match, Uncle Nate," Danielle Lynne mentioned, "I am going to take The Great Satan to Coral Grove, Sunday."

"To do the schooling show."

"Yeah, and I thought Eddie could do the flat classes when I did the over fences."

"And why would you sacrifice the show's championships, I mean why bother showing if you're not going for the championships?"

"Well, my goal here is just to school, see who is around here now, and Eddie just looks really good when he cantered over there."

"That he did," the teacher told his pupil, "that he did."

"Eddie, we have a proposition for you," Mr. Hawthorne, or Uncle Nate, shouted out.

Diamonds Are a Cheerleaders' Spectator Sport

Abigail, or Muffy as Eddie nicknamed her, watched Jake the Jock, spring formal date, throw some softball pitches to Truman Johnson during the weekend inter squad practice game that put the cheerleader's spring formal date on the same stage that he had been on since a child. But the spectator activity came to be a nice way to spend a sunny afternoon and not many took advantage of the free entertainment except for Peter, who clicked away at the exciting action that featured game-like conditions.

"He can pitch, he actually can pitch, Muffy," Peter chuckled as Abigail sat on the three-level bleacher.

"Oh, by the way, Peter, why did you and Eddie call me Muffy and Jake the Jock in the newspaper last semester?" Abigail questioned the journalist whom she had not seen since the spring.

"Well, Eddie needed to spend more time at the barn, you know, preparing for his second national championship and you were hanging out at the ball fields with Jake the Jock."

"Well," remembering how sweet Eddie was rescuing her from being stood up, "I am a free spirit."

"Well, so is Eddie," Peter clicked a smile as Abigail returned a photogenic smile.

Then the two focused in on the pretend battle between pitcher and batter, noticing the battery was starting to be a fine tune for the winter season.

Bearing Resemblance

Unlike Eddie Patrick and Danielle Lynne, the nursing student granted was still practicing her trade, but she was in a real life situation, walking the floor called pediatrics.

Seeing a young boy trying to use metal crutches reminded her of the way Eddie got around on campus. Just like an animal the aides acted like two extra legs to assist in the process of going from point A to point B.

"What a strange word 'aides'," the sophomore started to understand by spending a minute reflecting on the word when it is spoken not written, "they now have a disease called 'aids', we are being warned about it to the point it is scary, yet those canes are called aides too."

With the two words sounding alike despite being spelled differently, it was interesting to ponder the point that aides also included what the press secretary who was shot during President Reagan's assassination attempt had on staff.

Reflecting back on the crutches and Eddie using canes, another point came to mind that a synonym to 'cane' is 'staff'.

That is right: a disability can come at you in seconds, one day you are walking out of a plush hotel next to the most powerful person in the country. Then the next second you may not be able to speak or communicate a word despite being a press secretary. Yet, he was an aide to the leader of the country and now today he uses aides.

Bobbi Barnes, who had a male sounding name, observed the football player as she struggled like a smaller lineman trying to take down a running back.

Even he had everybody watching when he got hurt, Bobbi concluded about the injured patient.

Patient Student

It is like a grandmother's rocking chair, Eddie thought when he went into the canter by pressing his weak outside leg while pulling the reign toward the rail. All it took was a cluck and The Great Satan picked up the message in a clear, concise fashion. Having the instincts that the rider above him was a little bit different, the chestnut wanted to act a little bit more special, so every time he felt him losing his balance he would push him back to make it look very smooth.

With all the gookety gook gone, Danielle Lynne just smiled, watching the motion look so perfect when her horse went into the storybook style image that she loved to watch.

"Okay, now I want you to sit back in the saddle and pull back on the reigns," Mr. Hawthorne suggested, leaning on the rail.

And just like that, The Great Satan protected her mount, making a smooth transition back to the walk. Eddie felt his leg muscles squeeze as he straightened his back in the fun exercise that challenged the level no therapeutic round ball could ever reach. Both the trainer and his niece watched their rider for a couple seconds sit back, enjoying the merry-go-round sensation. Knowing Eddie, the therapeutic stimulation rivalry was good for the experienced equestrian.

"His back is just like yours and he has that weak leg just like you have," Mr. Hawthorne noted to Danielle Lynne.

"That he does. Hey, hot shot, are you buying me dinner on the way home?"

Taken back by the question posed and trying to gain his breath back in a fraction of a second, the thought that girl asked him on a date. Maybe it was just being in a barn, finally after all these years, and having a trusting comfortable feeling on the weekend afternoon.

Pulling a twenty out, Mr. Hawthorne gave it to Danielle Lynne, "Why don't you two go to TJ's down the road?"

"Hmm, do you want us to bring something back?"

"No, Angel cooked a couple steaks before leaving for the track; I can nuke them in the microwave."

"Oh, then we are going to head on back to school then. Eddie, you are driving me home, right?"

"Sure," Eddie squeaked, finally catching his breath.

"Look, I will help you off then we will do the saddle and reigns later."

"I can handle that," Uncle Nate encouraged them to go out and socialize.

"Yeah, I am hungry, you sure you do not want to join us, Uncle Nate?"

"No, that is all right; I will clean Angel Damian's saddle while you all get back to school."

It only took a few minutes for Danielle Lynne to wash down her horse. Besides able-bodied people doing things faster, she knew the cool down points of her friend. When all was concluded, The Great Satan was released into the field to enjoy his happy hour while the trio headed up to the house and cars. Danielle Lynne showed Eddie her gookety gook hands like they were covered with evil, alien space, monster blood when they got into the car, starting to lower their emotional guards when the honest barn kinship started to develop in a way where honesty was the key factor.

Recruitment Drive

When Peter got back from the office, he screened the phone machine which only had a few messages on this Saturday afternoon, including one from Bobbi reminding him to take shots at the recruitment day for the nursing school.

Bobbi is an interesting character on the campus, the reporter thought.

Her mother was the nurse while the father handled the finances by having one of those secure South Florida positions. They lived in a nice neighborhood her parents invested in when the area residents were alligators.

They were in the same social age group despite going to different schools and he knew her from afar or the numerous continuous mall trips. After their thirteen-year commitment inside the South Florida education system, she walked into the Freshman Orientation class when he was talking to this interesting person that was from New Jersey. He had the most outgoing personality, he noted, when they were discussing sports. Bobbi waltzed in with her golden blond hair looking like a professional, and taking the seat in front of the two journalists, she chuckled that the kid from the pizza parlor was going to the same school she was attending.

Pizza and then she was off to being a candy striper, Peter remembered looking through the negative file from last year's nursing recruitment exercise whose pictures were taken last spring by somebody who graduated, 'always busy'.

After throwing the dough around, he got that journalistic bug, taking a summer job at the local newspaper where he was keeping a busy schedule in the same mode that she did, only they never talked or saw each other until arriving on campus.

Perusing the still images that made a historical point on the timeline, he noted his generation was growing up, no longer were they being spoon-fed; instead, they, on their own, were wanting to be the ones taking on the responsibilities.

Picking up his photographer's bag, he decided to head back out and grab dinner when Danielle Lynne and Eddie were getting seated at TJ's. And she was ready to pop the offer to her classmate that on a horse she watched a handicap disappear.

Respectable Relationship Skills

"It is really nice to have a ride to the stable to see my horse," Danielle Lynne stated, sitting by Eddie who seemed to be taking this new adjustment pretty well, "I appreciate it."

Noticing they were both wearing britches and boots, the waitress came over in a sensitive way, waiting for the right opportunity not to bother them during a conversation.

"Can I take your order?"

They both smiled and ordered hamburgers with cheese with the young lady jotting things down like Peter did when writing a news story.

When she left the table, the verbal engagement started up again with them talking about Eddie's major which was called communication arts. Or better known as: 'How to turn on a Television Set'. An even a better description might be: 'Open Your Mouth and Speak'. But

Eddie was a little different when he described the urge to want people to know him who really did not know him.

Danielle Lynne had an opposite upbringing: her parents were at the horse shows, The Great Satan was the main focus of her ribbon collection and the only thing on her mind besides getting through high school was picking up the points to go to Harrisburg followed by New York City.

Once again, for some reason, they made it to the Tri State regional, but when they were ready to cut down to the final numbers that would go on to compete against all the other zones, The Great Satan would do something that would make her trainer define the weekend as a 'learning experience'.

They both heard the commotion when a couple kids dressed in the same tan pants that they were wearing entered into the restaurant and saw Danielle Lynne sitting at the table.

"It's Danielle Lynne, she actually came down to Florida," they shrieked, making her chuckle, "I wonder if she brought The Great Satan!!"

"It's the other barn, Eddie," Danielle Lynne smirked, holding the soda can at the top, "they love The Great Satan."

"Hey, Miss Danielle Lynne, is The Great Satan here?" one of them inquired.

"Yes, he arrived before I did. And how are you doing, Denise?"

As Denise, who had red freckles and an innocent pony tail, admired the substitute teacher, her mother came behind her with two hands on her shoulder.

"Thank you, Danielle Lynne, for that lesson you gave Denise a few years back the last time you were down here."

"Yeah, Eddie, before I graduated from high school I took a cruise, spent the weekend at Uncle Nate's and picked up ten bucks by giving a lesson."

"She still remembers all you taught her about focusing on the blue marking on the fence and never to look down or be down," the mother commented.

With a shrug of a head and smile, Danielle Lynne started the laughter which ended when the mother lured her daughter to the table where her brother was sitting. "That's Danielle Lynne and The Great Satan; they are going to ride in Europe in big shows one day," the little girl could be heard going to the rest of her family.

Returning to the date, business engagement, or meal with her class/barn mate, where the conversation pertaining to horse shows in South Florida was the main agenda, Danielle Lynne hit the twenty-year-old college sophomore that he was really going to enjoy something that he always wanted to experience.

Danielle Lynne would compete in the over fences classes at the smaller shows, while he then, like a stunt double, would enter as an exhibitor doing the flat competition. It was like sharing The Great Satan to bring home the ribbons.

Things are starting out really positive this semester, Eddie thought, *a female friend, a horse, and a goal.*

Medal Scripture

Mr. Hawthorne went up the wooden staircase into the second level to the tack room and it really hit him that

Angel Damian finally walked out. Things were going to change. Granted Danielle Lynne was finally down here with some direction, hopefully taking on the academic challenges that would steer her in the right direction.

There was Angel Damian's saddle sitting where Danielle Lynne placed it when Eddie's lesson finished. Finding the saddle soap, which his sister's daughter referred to as gookety gook, was pretty easy but then it was time to go into his show trunk to pull out the magical spray. This was no ordinary leather spray; instead, it had a secret ingredient that would make the rider look better when on the horse. In addition to the contents, there was the traditional bribing of the carrots that takes place upon the student's arrival and departure to the horse.

Cleaning the equipment was such a soothing experience to Nate and during this time of meditation the decision to take Angel Damian's metal strip off only to replace it with a new one.

Only a clock ticking made a sound when the trainer made sure the tack was clean while memories came back, including the first time Angel Damian came to the barn to ride. It wasn't the time on the horse that motivated her instead, she enjoyed just being around the animals, making sure they had everything all together and were settled comfortably. But, her riding dreams led her across the town to the rodeo when she was a young teenager where she studied barrel racing. She loved to go quick but always respected the true genesis to the trade. Nate was going to miss Angel Damian but knew they were going to get by despite the two hands missing.

With the saddle glistening in the darkness with only the tack room light shining down on it, the occasion had come to start a new era. Sitting at the engraving table, he placed the golden plate into the machine and typed in the lettering, 'EDDIE PATRICK'.

"Welcome to the world of show riding, Eddie Patrick, at the North South County Stables," Nathaniel Hawthorne recalled, sitting behind the typewriter contraption that made this golden metal piece a little bit more elegant.

Experimenting in Equitation

Danielle Lynne was now in the power seat for the couple miles down the road to the show grounds for the schooling competition designed to test green horses and allow beginners like Eddie to work in a ring.

Since The Great Satan needed special treatment due to attitude problems, it was Danielle Lynne's responsibility to stay back and the final load to go over to the housing developments that had the nice complex that was equipped to host these exhibiting competitions.

Eddie, with his sports jacket and tie hanging in the back of his car, trucked over some of the kids who were looking to take down some other barns in the equestrian community gathering. Not even a father yet, Eddie heard all the childish conversations about how certain other stable riders didn't have a chance in the over fences classes.

A horse show was really easy to understand, only thing, it was very time consuming while the nerves tested seemed to tie a stomach in knots to the point where those insides felt queasy. Despite spending time during his freshmen year at the barn, this was the first able-bodied experience and there was no difference to what he experienced back in the northeast than down south.

"Hey, Eddie," Danielle Lynne yelped, jumping out of the truck and walking to the back trailer to unleash The Great Satan from her standing room, only area that had the chestnut princess take up two seats.

Eddie heard her a bit and maneuvered on the uneven ground as the children fixed their hairnet and hooked on their exhibitor numbers, all commenting that they were not really in a competition instead, they were showing off their horses to the other barns.

"Yeah, look at our perfect horse, you wish yours was like mine, well, you know it isn't," they chattered in a satirical way that rivaled little league baseball.

"Hey, Eddie," Danielle Lynne screeched a little louder, this time holding a bridle-less chestnut with a nylon rope with a golden inscription 'The Great Satan' on it that was doused with gookety gook.

This time Eddie heard the cries for help and headed over to assist in any way possible.

"Here, Eddie," Danielle Lynne said, giving him the blue nylon rope with the golden inscription 'The Great Satan'.

"I am starving and I need to get some breakfast and register for my classes."

While all this interaction with the disabled person was unfolding, the children stood there with their helmets on and chinstraps dangling wanting to be hooked, giggling at the move Miss Danielle Lynne made on the national champion at the walk with a leader but no side walker, of course, but a blue ribbon with a trophy is a blue ribbon and a trophy.

Just like Eddie, the kids made sure their horses were taken care of by holding them while they tried to enjoy the grass that was seasoned by moist dew that was like Caesar dressing on the salad for animals.

A Sunday Ritual

Looking over to the other bed, Bobbi noticed the spread was already down with nobody in it. Remembering it was Sunday, the nursing student went through a check list of what needed to be done today: church to brunch then to the library, followed by dinner and then back to the library. Not that this practice seemed strange but nothing was going to get in the way of her immediate goal right now, which was putting her feet on the ground to welcome the 'eight thirty in the morning' sunrise.

"Oh yeah, I have to get something ready for Peter and the recruitment drive tomorrow, cheese the weese," she said with a yawn.

'Oh, around eight thirty-five in the morning, Miss Danielle Lynne', as the young riders called her, had her breakfast, which consisted of a donut, in her mouth and her other hand was tightening the girth of a beginner rider ready to challenge a five fence hunter course.

"Let's see, one, two into the middle, four, five," the rider, who was still learning penmanship and how to count to ten, studied the course with the same intense thought that Eddie had while taking his finals last spring.

"That is exactly right, just like we did in the ring yesterday."

Putting her munchkin hands over the gigantic reins, the youngster took charge of the situation in a professional manner like a CEO reviewing their troops.

"Walk on, Sebastian," she said and the small pony knew something was up, so it did as it was told by perking up its ears then marching forward to the in gate.

Still with a white clean shirt on which only had jelly spot that the jacket would cover, the dirt from the ground had not penetrated the situation and more importantly Jessica McCord was prepared at the gate. .

"That is right, Jessica," Miss Danielle Lynne barked out as the grammar school motioned a 'hello' to her mother, who was wearing a University of Miami tee shirt "C'mon now, pay attention."

And into a canter she went, reminding Sebastian who was in control.

Staring at the first jump, the two blooped over the x obstacle like her brother's little league baseball team getting lucky when hitting the ball.

"Whoa, easy," could be heard along with an attempt to make sure all her strides were being counted properly.

Chuckling, the judge scribbled something on a piece of paper and when she looked up from her box 'Oh, oh' came out of her mouth.

Following that premonition, the small pony missed the third fence and headed into the ring, coming to a complete stop like someone hit the brakes on the car. At that moment, the half dozen people around the ring could hear in a loud voice, "Sebastian!!"

Then the next second, the scene unfolded as Jessica naturally gripped her legs to the saddle, sat back, and felt the foot drive hard, making her heel start an 'L' shape.

"Sebastian!!" was now a growl and Jessica finally loosened the reigns and made her way to the top of the line.

"That is all right," Miss Danielle Lynne assured her, "the important thing is you did not fall off."

Being more concentrated on the line or two fences in front of her, Jessica heard Miss Danielle Lynne but seemed more concentrated so it went in one ear, registered and then went out the other ear.

Back in total control, she hit the fence straight on, counted the proper strides to the next little X then finished the round with a resounding, "Sebastian, good boy."

"That was good," Miss Danielle Lynne grabbed the bridle, leading Jessica outside the ring, allowing her classmate from another barn to go inside to try her luck.

"All right, you are not going to get a ribbon this morning, but the main point is you did not blow your cool and stayed on Sebastian, showing everybody around the ring you do not panic," Miss Danielle explained, "hey, a ribbon costs about a dollar and it does look pretty on the wall but the lesson you learned today was worth a million dollars."

"A million dollars?" she asked as her classmate pony did the same thing at the same fence.

"Yeah, the horses are teaching you something, you know they talk through telekinesis to each other and then they whinny to emphasize a point."

"What's tele whatever?" Jessica returned with a question.

"Well, it is a magical time when no one talks, only use their minds to send a message and Sebastian and the other pony probably chit chatted last night so their friends would learn a lesson."

"Is that true? Sebastian, did you call up Hurricane and plan this whole thing?" Jessica laughed while Sebastian gave a small snort when they returned to the makeshift barn that resembled trailers.

"Now, Jessica, your other class is not until this afternoon, I want you to get a bite to eat then watch me jump The Great Satan, then it will be your turn to go."

"Yes, Miss Danielle Lynne," Jessica remarked, jumping off the pony to the ground.

"Thank you, Danielle Lynne," Jessica's mother stated, "she'll be fine."

Still holding Sebastian, the mother watched her child prance through the grass to see her friend from school.

"Courtney, Sebastian and Hurricane were on the phone last night and...," Danielle Lynne watched until her voice drowned out and she knew it was almost ready for her first class.

"Eddie, good morning,"

"Here, hold this for a second," Danielle Lynne gave the reins to her future chauffer.

Sunday Studies and Library Lectures

Abigail came out of the elevator and saw blond-headed Bobbi sitting at a table, and the dark-haired cheerleader walked over to ask a question from the nursing student.

"Have you seen Eddie?" Abigail stated.

"He is at a horse competition and so is my roommate."

"Your roommate is at a horse competition thing with Eddie?" Abigail, a little stunned, retorted.

"Yeah, Danielle Lynne is my roommate and she owns a horse and Eddie rides it too, something like that."

"Something like that?" Bobbi could hear, watching Abigail, trying not to laugh.

"Oh, I just wanted to go over with him the facts I wanted him to take down in his notebook at practice."

Holding back the question, "You have practice?" Bobbi minded her Catholic pees and cues by trying not to laugh.

"Nope, they won't be back until tonight, and that reminds me I have to see Peter about the photos he is going to take at our recruitment drive tomorrow."

"Is that for your nursing thing?"

"Have you even chosen a major? You know nursing is not a bad job?"

"Huh, you are starting to sound like my parents and no, I have no idea what I am going to do with the rest of my life."

"Oh."

"Well, anyway, got to run, duty calls."

"You have your leotards on."

"That is not until later tonight, right now I have got to find out how the Fish Sticks are doing in the football game."

"They play tomorrow night."

"Oh yeah, well, I am off to do something."

"Find some structure, Abbey, besides writing love letters to your boyfriend at Notre Dame."

"Okay, Mom," was Abigail's response.

Small Stalls Opening Big Doors

Far away and a couple miles down the road from the half a dozen people cheering their love ones on, Angel Damian pitchforked another gigantic brown thing and threw it into a wheel barrel.

As the claiming horse took a break from his feed bucket, the contractual worker admired the housekeeper's work and tried not to interfere, despite the fact that small one's open air room could barely fit the two dedicated professionals.

Opening the stall door, Angel wheeled the contents outside only to remind the claimer that rent was due at the end of the month, or he will find himself in a pasture of green unlike the road side bar that was filled by the race track residents across the street.

"Angel, you hunter/jumper you, I need you to work a few horses out tomorrow; can you come out here a little early?" the overweight individual said, wearing his license on his shirt.

Apparently, the trainer had made some contacts bringing some more talent onto the stage and did not realize they needed some seasoning before the performance.

"Sure, Mr. Walt," Angel Damian said with a smile.

"My assistant trainer Donald will be here to guide you."

Mr. Walt seemed to be a genuinely nice person always giving like Nate Hawthorne at North/South County Stables. And his pay was very good and of course on Monday, the track was dark just like today so after dumping the hay full of dirty horse linens she could go back home to get some sleep. Since Monday morning, this quarterback would assist in the decision making.

Rubber Stamped and Approved to Go

Both Danielle Lynne and Eddie Patrick mirrored each other, wearing the same jacket and brown tan jodhpurs along with black boots with the only difference being the flat rider needed the rubber version while the over fences competitor wore the traditional leather.

Smiling, Mr. Hawthorne carried the saddle which now had the golden name plate 'Eddie Patrick' and the magical spray that will make the rider's back as straight as an arrow.

"I wish you could be both in leather riding boots," Uncle Nate seemed relaxed.

"Well, Uncle Nate, Eddie will not let go of the rubber kind."

"Nate, they never could get the zipper to go that far down and I cannot pull a leather boot on," Eddie interrupted as Danielle Lynne giggled.

"Me first," she said, mounting The Great Satan from the ground and pranced him to the show ring as both the trainer and Eddie followed.

"Don't fall off," Eddie sarcastically quipped and she just looked back.

"Just worry about driving me home with some colorful additions to my dorm room."

Continuing into the ring, she motioned to the gate keeper that it was her turn and started to gracefully break into a short trot followed by a nice easy canter. Using her eyes, all Danielle Lynne could think about was the easy eight fence course; after making the introductory circle, she was straight on for the first one which was nice and flowing.

The traditional "Easy, Danielle" came from the in gate as her Uncle watched on with Eddie Patrick studying the body structure.

Not flinching her mind, the next fence immediately came to be a reality then a memory as the two had no problem dealing with the equine obstacle course. Time to go into the ring's middle for a single effort, which meant watching the corner then slowly turning her head to go down the line like a dressage horse wanting to dance to the center imaginary 'X' mark. Needing to know where exactly she was without making a production, the cool motionless picture jumped the middle set, perfectly followed by the final line. Hitting the final mark was an accomplishment and the half dozen people actually watching the feat clapped.

A little out of breath, she trotted back to the in gate where the son of show committee member wearing shorts asked the next question.

"Miss Danielle Lynne, would you like to do your next course?"

"Yeah, sure," she replied.

And the next three to five minutes, Danielle Lynne accomplished the encore through some nice jumping efforts which created positive grades on the judge's card.

Her mother Jessica watched the two rounds in between feasting on clams casino and linguini.

"Danielle Lynne is such a beautiful rider," the youngster said.

"What was that?" her mother replied, putting down Sun Sentinel for a minute.

"Danielle Lynne," Jessica paused, "is such a beautiful rider."

"And you know why?"

"Concentration like when you are in school," her mother felt it was time for a quick conversation since the subject seemed to ooze out in a tranquil setting, "if you stay focused on what is going on, you will learn."

"You mean no more daydreaming about Sebastian?"

"No, day dreaming is fine since that only means you have things to daydream about, but when you are in the classroom course you have to be attentive to what the teacher is doing."

"It is just like falling off," watching her daughter spin the pasta on the fork, and before putting lunch in her mouth Jessica responded, "if I lose concentration on Sebastian then I will lose my balance and fall off, if I lose my concentration when Mrs. Apple is talking about my time table then I will not hear the information and will fall off, right?"

"Right."

"You're next, hot shot," the positive Danielle Lynne said, hopping off The Great Satan.

"There are about three more horses to go in the over fences classes so that gives us about fifteen minutes until the flat class," Eddie was standing there ready to go, wanting to go into the schooling area as Danielle Lynne dismounted.

Already, a couple of the barn kids had their orders from Miss Danielle Lynne to stand at each corner of the ring and watch Eddie to make sure he was on the proper diagonal. The Great Satan peered over to the two canes, keeping the individual up, knowing that he was going to push him into working his inner leg.

"We are going to give it our best shot," she told him, placing the blue ladder they brought from the barn. Once aboard, the barn trekked over to the schooling area, working as a team to show off what they had been doing all week while others outside the equestrian world simply ate potatoe chips while watching *General Hospital.* Danielle Lynne let her chauffer go into the schooling area to warm up for the big event, Eddie Patrick's first show class against able-bodied people.

Structured Course Syllabus

Shorts on and the leotard top showcasing the cheerleader's southern Florida charm, Abigail skipped across campus, trying to find something structural to fill the void which the laid back atmosphere tempted her on the early fall weekend.

Had the brunch, went to church then back home, okay, there is that I could do, too bored to lay out in the sun. In a couple seconds, she confessed to herself by turning around to head across the pathway back to the library with identification in hand.

"All right, Sister, I will go back and read Chapters 2–3 of *Teaching to Children: On Your Level.*"

Heading right back up the stairs into the air-conditioned library, she went straight to the elevator where Bobbi was drowning in texts.

"See, you came back for some structure," Bobbi giggled to the sorority sister who just wanted to have fun.

"Yeah, I am back to get some structure, as you put it."

"Very good, Abigail, now go over there and sit down to read your book," the committed nursing student told Abigail who could be defined by traditional serious students as, 'I really do not have a major so I will write down education to shut everybody up'.

Sitting down, she saw Bobbi continue to play with her blond hair as Abigail's dark hair started to be more attractive when the pages to the book started honestly on Chapter 2.

Bobbi could read the title of the publication *Teaching to Children: On Your Level,* and the perfect grader had to take a break for a trip to the water fountain which was situated right by Abigail's study location.

"*Teaching to Children: On Your Level?*" The sarcastic health care academic questioned.

"Yes, it is a very interesting read and if I did not have a test on Thursday this would not really interest me."

"Really, Abigail, I would think children or especially teenagers would be able to take away a lot from your life experiences."

"I suppose," Abigail commented back as Bobbi filled her mouth, followed by a jug of water, "but I am not ready for all this serious stuff. Does everything come with a catch?"

"No."

"First off, you're in grammar school, everything is like controlled then comes high school, you do not have a car, then you have a car, you like someone, you love someone, then you say good bye to them so you can take your car off to college so you can be an adult, then you have responsibilities, bills, when does it ever end?"

"When it hits the fan," Bobbi snickered, walking back to her books which she was studying like every Sunday night when the four o'clock football games were on television.

"Oh, by the way, Bobbi, when you told me to sit over here that is not the right way to talk to a child, in fact, you can scar them for life if you do not use care."

"Is this when the child is in a controlled situation?"

"When does a child not have a controlled environment?"

"That is when they get into trouble and that is why you need…"

"Structure,"

"Abigail, you have not changed since high school."

"I no longer have him and well I have a car on campus."

"Oh yeah, him."

A few hours passed and around the time Danielle Lynne was putting The Great Satan to bed while Eddie had the colored ribbons on the front seat, Bobbi looked up, decided to call it a night and go over what needed to be known tomorrow. At the same time, the cheerleader did the same thing and noticing they missed the cafeteria food, it was time to take Abigail's car to find somewhere else to eat.

"I thought you had something to do with that sexy leotard?" Bobbi asked.

Looking straight in her eye, "I just realized something: I have a car, I have friends, it is not snowing outside and yes, I know what I am studying."

"That is what structure will do for you."

Class Work

With the kids all standing guard in a way that a disability should be handled, no one noticed them showing support for their barn mate as the college student with a tremendous weak leg struggled to push up and down.

Out of the corner of his eye, Eddie watched them shake their head 'yes' when he picked up the proper motion that would be tasteful to the judge. Still requesting a trot, Eddie could feel the tension create an environment that seemed to attack his endurance. Or maybe it was just a weird form of stage fright, knowing there were a dozen people watching you take a test.

Around the second bend, the horse rider combination on the surface seemed to be an altogether package despite the bouncy sensation called a trot started to be taxing.

Then it happened and it was coming from a fourth grader who was still trying to spell the name 'Christopher Columbus'. She shook her head side to side, signifying that Eddie needed to sit on the saddle for a split second then pop right back up.

Well, there goes the red or blue ribbon, the thought quickly flashed into his mind since this exhibitive competition did not have a three strike rule.

Just like at the barn, the cantering portion still had the relaxed rocking chair feeling that was very soothing to the children at the rail doing their job by assisting their chauffer in this monumental occasion.

After they played out the same scene in the direction, the judge requested the four individuals to come into the middle ring to receive their grades. Granted if Danielle Lynne did the class which Eddie handled, the under saddle assignment they would have another championship with a plastic silver thing that would need to be polished every so often, but that was not the case since the talented individual stepped away to allow the undergraduates to spend some time in the spotlight.

Jessica came over to the in gate where Danielle Lynne was standing holding a blue, red, and white ribbon. While still watching Eddie, Sebastian's best friend handed her the red and white ones and The Great Satan came off the stage with a green one when Danielle Lynne looked down.

"What are these?"

"Your ribbons," Jessica replied, looking up with the black gloves covering up her small hands while holding tightly to the blue one.

"What about the other one?" Danielle Lynne asked.

"That is Sebastian's; he did a really good job, the judge came by the restaurant and told me."

She smiled, which turned to a laugh as Eddie came through the gate.

"Judge said Jessica did a good job."

"Sebastian did a good job."

"Oh, that is great," retorted Eddie, feeling very comfortable he was around friends.

It only took a few minutes to get back as Danielle Lynne, in her hand, had the red, white, and green ribbons.

"I wonder if this means anything," Danielle Lynne said while helping Eddie's leg over the saddle.

"I think it means we are stopping for Italian on the way home," her chauffer replied, "I'm hungry."

When Jessica went to put her saddle into the back of the truck, the older six graders put their red and white ribbon up against Sebastian's blue.

"I guess we are going to have French tonight."

"French, yuck, I want Irish," the other came back, bringing Eddie's ribbon over to the group, "yeah, Irish, you know like Mick Dees."

Looking collegiate, Abigail stood next to her new best friend and old high school classmate Bobbi as a tired looking Danielle Lynne came stumbling down the hallway, dragging the brown dock shoes she was wearing with dark socks pulled up to her thigh.

Bobbi kept the door and had her hand on the knob, slowly letting it creek open, and the equestrian barely made it to her bed before she collapsed like it was the final feet to relaxation.

"I do not remember Eddie being that good," Abigail snickered.

"No," Bobbi sort of mouthed.

Across campus, Eddie was still wide awake while the Big Mac taste lingered in his mouth and watching the priest prepare Holy Communion in the student hall for the late mass, this was his main course followed by sugar bread cookies.

Autumn Classic Nights with New Hope

Autumn Classic, as Danielle Lynne nicknamed her, learned a tremendous amount riding in the fall schooling shows. But she did not achieve her goal of beating Sebastian while her bedroom had a colorful interior decoration created by New Hope. When the two exhibited, as Mr. Hawthorne used to explain to them at

105

the Thanksgiving Show, she held her own and was very happy with the results. In fact, the Saturday Night mini prix event was so big that Danielle Lynne returned from the Thanksgiving dinner up north to compete in it, and she planned an experiment that made other members in the hunter/jumper organization interpret it as the true meaning of the holiday.

After going clean and qualifying for the jump off in the evening class touted as the marquee event to the weekend Equestrian tradition, Danielle Lynne stepped away from the schooling area since she was already prepared for the jump off to allow Eddie Patrick and Mr. Hawthorne to showcase a disabled riding demonstration.

Purposely, Mr. Hawthorne worked around the jump crew on stage, changing the course and the obstacles in the same way the theatrical stage moves scenery for the next act. With rags at their sides, both Autumn and Mischa performed as the side walkers who disappeared quietly like a ballerina giving up the spotlight to the star. Despite being second in the deciding round, Danielle Lynne gripped the lead line very loosely as a leader allowing the large pony with a big heart to prove why he had a wide range in showmanship.

In the same way the ballet partner would give way to the principal dancer, Danielle Lynne unhooked the rope to give the stage up to Eddie but continued to look the part while smiling at Eddie with the message, *Don't you dare fall off.* Nothing earth shattering happened; instead, leaning up against the metal in gate that opens when someone wants to enter into the ring, Danielle Lynne watched him gracefully go into the rocking chair style cantor. Coming to a smooth transition, which meant his time being the most important thing to pay attention too was finished, the show photographer documented the happening by clicking with the camera. As everybody applauded, his barn was at the in gate, ready to assist Eddie off the mount while getting The Great Satan ready for the jump off. To add to the success using the same saddle with the magical ingredient, Danielle Lynne ended up pinning in her first mini prix.

After that hard working evening, the barn dined on cheese pizza and in County Line Stable tradition mayonnaise was placed on the Italian dining experience.

When the bird finished its stay in the refrigerator, courtesy of the visiting relatives in between going back to school, the lights to the Christmas tree decorated the South Florida landscape despite the weather not calling for snow.

About a week before Danielle Lynne and Eddie Patrick headed back north, the kids had their day at the yearly banquet at the Fort Lauderdale hotel. In ball like fashion, Autumn Barton and Mischa Taylor met up with Jessica McCord in the bathroom. "So, are all the mothers done saying wow? You all look nice out of your riding clothes," Mischa complained while Jessica McCord searched her pocket book for her lipstick.

"Actually, my mom thinks I am going to the prom."

"Really, Jessica, I thought you would already be doing photoshoots for First Holy Communion dresses," Autumn snickered as they left the bathroom.

"Modeling is not everything it is cracked up to be," Jessica retorted as the door opened to reveal their parents.

"Hi, Mom," they all shrieked.

"All ready for the roast beef and mash potatoes."

Food for Thought in a Showplace to Be Rich

A long way from the formal dinner where the children all dressed up, Angel Damian sat in a booth with a roast beef sandwich filled with mayonnaise on the top and bottom. It was soft and her body was still burning from the workout that she had all day.

"Things went well today," she whispered out as the small lights flickered above the offices on the South Beach Down's backstretch.

She had one show and one in the place position, which must have been a message to the trainers that her tactics overseeing the horses were caring, and she knew the special carrots that were slipped to them before heading to the paddock had a magical aura giving the long shots new hope.

"Had the five horse," a white uniform man came over to her after cleaning up after the dinner crowd.

"Excuse me?"

"In seventh race, Mr. Walt's horse, the five," he repeated.

"Oh yeah, they picked her up really quickly and Mr. Walt gave me an extra in my daily pay check."

"There were rumors all over the backstretch that there was going to be some interest in the claim box," the gentlemen told the exercise rider/groom/hot walker, "ran over there on my break and placed a twenty."

"Angel Damian," she wiped the mayonnaise off her fingers.

"Keith," the backstretch cook know with an outstretched arm mentioned, "some of the jocks and jockettes call me chef de Keith, those who know how to ride other than around barrels."

"Oh, I am so over that dream," Angel reminded herself.

"What dream?"

"The redcoats and going back to the northeast to show the world I have the right image,"

"Right image," Chef de Keith responded.

"To you know…"

"To what?"

Angel looked at him as his cooking style came through and in true fashion, "You get what you put into the mix."

"If you ride a claimer, it is a claimer, if you ride an allowance horse, it is an allowance horse, and—"

"A stakes horse may be rare but wherever it finishes, it goes down good," the two laughed, knowing that the big races come once in a while like visiting that table cloth restaurant on the beach front strip.

And when the laughter was over, Chef de Keith spoke up with one more line in the late evening scene, "Remember, do not bet your lunch money because you always need something to put into the mix."

"Yes, Chef de Keith, they tell me that every time I give them a carrot or apple it's the show pool that benefits."

Knowing When to Kick and When to Have a Quiet Seat

The calendar on the wall now read 1986 and Mr. Hawthorne sat in the feed room which had a desk and a chair.

He could hear Autumn quietly giggling with Mischa, "Do you think Eddie 'The National Champion' and Miss

Danielle Lynne 'The Olympian' would mind if we take The Great Satan for a spin around the ring?"

Mischa just looked at Autumn with a stare, "Autumn, you have something that both Danielle Lynne and Eddie do not have," she tried to remind her in a nice way.

Mr. Hawthorne was able to hear the whole conversation and wondered to himself if he should walk out to interject his own opinion on the situation.

"What do you mean I have something that Danielle Lynne and Eddie do not have?" Autumn inquired, putting a foot in the stirrup and vaulting onto The Great Satan.

Mischa kept her mouth shut as her friend took The Great Satan into the ring and walked around the gigantic oval circle.

"So, Mischa, why didn't you tell Autumn what she had that my niece did not?"

Mischa looked at her watch and the second hand, and started a countdown, "Fifteen," pause, "Ten," another pause, "Five," a pause a third time, "Four, three, two, one."

"Are you all right, Autumn?" Mr. Hawthorne took his pipe out of his mouth.

"Right on schedule," Mischa added.

Claiming the Proper Baggage

"C'mon, Eddie,"

"What? Our bags are going to be there when we get to baggage claim."

"Stop talking, you know I cannot talk and walk at the same time."

As the two riders left the Piedmont Airlines flight, Mr. Hawthorne stood outside the gate, waiting to pick up his two star clients.

"Welcome back," he shouted when they were in sight.

"Uncle Nate," Danielle Lynne responded.

After the hugs, they all headed downstairs to the conveniently located baggage claim at the Fort Lauderdale Airport.

While Eddie was watching for the bags, Mr. Hawthorne took his niece aside and smiled, "It is really nice to have you back."

"I sort of missed it down here, went shopping in New York and went to the tree."

"Which of course now is with the combined training people," Uncle Nate continued to look happy during the conversation.

"Uncle Nate."

"Well, we missed you at the lighted boat parade."

"Maybe next year."

"Guess what?"

"What?"

"Earlier today…," Uncle Nate paused, "The Great Satan dumped the Autumn Classic."

Chuckling, Danielle Lynne commented, "It took her all this time to get on The Great Satan."

"I guess there is just new hope for her."

"They're here," a distant cry on two canes announced.

"Here, I will get them," Uncle Nate offered, "oh, Eddie, your car is safely parked in our lot."

Miles of Markers

As death settled its yearly vacation plans in the north, life still existed in the south when Straw sat behind the big steering wheel of the RV which acted as a business office in the parking position. Hitting the Florida State line, there was no more worry about foul weather or maybe a heavy thunderstorm. Since there were blue skies ahead that was not going to happen for the retired gentlemen looking to rest in peace during another snowbird season.

Watching the mile markers lowered in numbers and the Cypress Gardens advertisements turned east toward the soon- to-be studio city in Central Florida, Straw kept the course, waiting for the space coast to come into clear view. Heading across the desolate beeline was nothing new for the horse show photographer and the road seemed endless. Finally, when NASA took over the driver's attention, Straw knew the final leg to the trip was coming to a close.

In the back were files and developing equipment which would suspend eventful memories to be cherished forever in the buyer's mind. It was not the business aspect that was driving the extra miles; instead, artistic responsibility was the true reason behind the trip.

Finally, signs for West Palm Beach came into view with smaller ones noting the Show Grounds location. Only a few more minutes as the sun started to set then Straw would finally be able to lay down before cooking dinner in the compact kitchen inside the gigantic automobile.

Taking a left hand turn with great care, Straw drove very slowly until he met the guard standing by the gate.

"Straw, Happy New Year to you," the security guard said with a smile, "all your papers were in on time and you have the same reserved spot."

Looking the same as every other year, Straw watched the lonely show jumps canvas the different rings, "Another Southern Hospitality show season has started and a new year to boot."

Confirming Straw's smile was seeing the plot next to him already dressed up with a gigantic painting stating, 'Visions by Calfee'.

AA to BA to RN

Already registered for class, Bobbi Barnes peered through the glass to the newborn bassinettes that lined the hospital floor. One nurse came over and picked up the infant, and the second year nursing student watched like monitoring the professor giving a lecture in the hall.

Noticing how careful the professional performed her duties, Bobbi made a check list in her mental steno book concerning the event. Then all of a sudden, Eddie Patrick came to mind and it was not the mysterious arm bands that he wore on his wrists; instead, it was the true reason he walked in an odd fashion that forced him to use two canes.

Wearing her uniform with pride, Bobbi continued to watch the child be placed ever so softly in the sterilized crib. Moving away from the window, she walked down the aisle filled with lightly colored walls engulfed by the white fluorescent lights above her head. All of a sudden, Sister Remick, a nun at the Catholic Hospital, came out of nowhere and nearly bumped into Bobbi, which made her take a step back.

"Sister," Bobbi smiled.

"I noticed you watching the newborns," said Sister Remick.

"Yes, I am getting ready to register for classes and…"

"Getting some extra credit?"

"Yeah, wearing the uniform in case they need me to do something and show how hard I work."

"Just remember, work may be counted in hours but the time you spend could change someone's life forever," the Sister Remick in the black-and-white attire stated.

Parting Bobbi pondered on her last lesson and soon, Eddie Patrick came back, into her memory *What did happen to Eddie Patrick?*

Setting the Backstage Scene

"She made it through first semester," Straw came out of his portable photography studio on wheels to meet the artist in his mobile studio.

Chuckling to himself, he could still remember how she fell in love with The Great Satan when their barn sold the girl the pony at a very low cost. "She was so frustrated on those huge horses," he smiled, "but when The Great Satan allowed her into his life the partnership it was like magic."

As both elder gentlemen worked like elves at Santa's workshop, their business locations made the plots on the county ground which was not commercial property instead, elegant boutiques that had a picture book presence.

"That is right, Straw," Calfee pondered when everything was set up, "we are here for two months not one week and we are here to add to the dream like setting and if everything is classy then the money will come."

Looking at his plant that really was a small piece that existed up north over two hundred years ago, Straw agreed.

"We create the dream and they have it to remember."

Home from the Holidays

When Eddie pulled into his designated spot on campus, he put the car into the proper gear and unhooked his seat belt. "Thanks for the ride, Eddie"

"You're welcome," Eddie replied, watching her disembark from the automobile.

Grabbing his two canes, he figured his bags could wait a few minutes to get the luggage and still felt uncomfortable asking a girl to do the job. It was not a power thing since he was a national champion in a sport where not only disabled can compete with the able-bodied on a socially acceptable level but men against woman also find a common ground in the show ring.

"Do you want me to get the luggage?" she asked.

"No, I am going to deal with all that later."

"Well, thanks for being there."

"You too, I will see you tomorrow."

Reporting for the Semester

He was shifting through photographs he took during the winter break, while the big school a few miles south of Southern Dominican Catholic University played their bowl game. He came across some nice shuts of the Orange Bowl when a knock came on the door.

"No one is here," he said, knowing it was Eddie, "I bought the Girl Scout cookies earlier this week, you're late."

Another knock on the door made Peter King put the pictures on the desk and go to open it, "I said you are not going to the Super Bowl."

"But…"

"No, they are not going to the Super Bowl."

"Neither are the Fish Sticks,"

"We went last year," his friend defended the only South Florida only professional franchise.

"And are people actually going to the games?"

"Well, that is a whole other story."

Both canes in hand, Eddie Patrick stepped into the office, "Sit there. Here, I will move the box of photographs."

Moving the black and whites was followed by Eddie taking the sticks in one hand, slowly sitting down.

"So, how was the vacation?"

"Christmas was good, New Years was the best I have ever had."

"You and Danielle Lynne went out?"

"Mostly every night we went to a couple horse shows together and gave a few lessons, you know Miss Danielle Lynne is home."

"What were the dates like?"

"They were fun, we did Christmas shopping together and I ended up over her house Christmas Day Night, then New Year's we went up to upstate New York to visit her family."

"Sounds like you had a busy time."

"So what is happening around here?"

"Board is starting to explore opportunities to build a gym."

Peter was at the meeting where the President and Athletic Director discussed in a public forum that consisted of just the school newspaper that a gym would finally get built on the campus. They promised it when the reporter was a freshman and this session was the first step in the process.

"No, gimpy, I did not ask anything about you getting a banner for the National Championship."

"Two National Championships," Eddie put up the peace sign, "baseball team zero."

Peter did not know how to say it so he just blurted it out, figuring Danielle Lynne is taking up most his time.

"Frank and Abigail got back together over the winter break."

"Really, I know she really likes that guy."

Jockette Looking to Jockey for Proper Position

"Okay, the car is still running and it will not need a tune up for the next few months," Angel Damian said to herself when she parked in the driveway to the rented apartment that overlooked the strip and beach. It was not the fact she was kicked out of the house or anything; instead, her handlers were able to put her up in a place that could be paid for by the income that she received at the track.

Next week was a test and she was still working with the information when studying the real life equine texts during the morning workouts. Mr. Walt had everything taken care of, and the claimer she was closest to was named *Lost Mountain:* a gelding that had great feedback when all alone on the track and it had only a few opportunities to showcase the talent. Winning the maiden put money in the owner's pocket and the second followed by a third was a great relief, but when it came to the fourth tryout, the owners still played the box line hoping no one would notice the horse.

After talking to Mr. Walt, they decided to give the hot walker a shot at cutting her teeth on the South Beach Downs dirt track at six furlongs.

Well, it wasn't a measly donation after a sunrise workout, she thought, opening the car door into the cool breeze air, *this was where all the snowbirds show up to watch the big purses, this was racing at South Beach Downs.*

Waking from the hot stone filled lot into the complex, she saw the water had a very nice white light reflection. They said the strip was going to make a big comeback when the revitalization was complete. Angel Damian never really knew what was wrong with the legendary oceanside community. Continuing tradition during the evening, the sidewalks were filled with those enjoying the social activity that had a backdrop including cars along with a thundering ocean.

Pulling her keys out of the pocket, she noticed Mrs. Coco with cane in hands meet Angel Damian at the rail.

"Did you get the rent money, Mrs. Coco?" Angel Damian asked.

"That is what I wanted to tell you, the room is all paid for through the meet."

"Mr. Walt…"

"Yeah, he said you are going to be a really good jockette," she said, "just like the other one."

"Caroline Crawford."

"Yeah, that was her name."

She said, taking the next few steps to the second level to the apartment complex that had a look of a seaside motel. When she reached the top, Angel Damian turned to see waves crash and the darkness shadowed by the traffic lights energized her, knowing the future held some really nice opportunities.

24/7

With her white collar prepped up, Bobbi Barnes reserved a table for Peter and Eddie as they entered into the twenty-four hour diner with the interesting staff.

"I have already ordered a grand slam, Peter," Bobbi mentioned as the two slid into the booth. Taking the outer side, Eddie placed the canes softly in the middle, bringing the traditional 11:30 pm down from the college scene set.

"Sorry, we were late, Eddie stopped by and we got to talking,"

"Hi, Eddie," she retorted as the waitress with the 'B-movie' look came over with the small steno pad in hand to take notes.

"Is there anything I can get you two?" she said as Bobbi made another line in her text book with a highlighter.

"Bacon and eggs," Peter responded to the question.

"Grilled cheese and tomato," Eddie followed.

"We are out of tomatoes," she reported back, "will an avocado do?"

Giving her a creative look, Eddie respectfully declined and decided just to have the cheese melted on toast.

Closing the text book, noticing her friends joined her for the late night dinner after work, Bobbi sat back and capped the yellow highlighter she was using to make the text so colorful.

"I tell you," Bobbi shook her head, "Eddie, how did you put up with all this…"

Eddie just stared at her with a quizzical look.

"The hospital."

"The hospital?" Eddie returned the question.

"Eddie, you were in the hospital?" Peter sarcastically added with Bobbi who just smiled.

"To tell you the truth I do not remember much, not even from my teenage life."

"You do not remember the nurses?" she questioned.

"Vaguely," he responded, "I do remember dark hallways with this yellow light and a dark figure going up and down."

"The nurse,"

"Yes, the nurse, and she is rolling a machine and comes in the room in the middle of the night just to take my blood pressure and take my temperature."

"They wake you up just to make you go back to sleep again," Bobbi stared at him.

"Actually, we used to get them back by hitting the red button."

Bobbi started to laugh.

"When we needed water."

"Have you ever kept up with your roommate?" the questioning nurse inquired.

"Actually, he died before I was discharged."

"He died?" Peter King joined the conversation.

"Bad heart."

And on that note, Bobbi sat back when the waitress brought the grand slam to her place, "Imagine that Bobbi," Eddie continued looking into her blue eyes and fluffed blonde hair, "the final things you will ever see with the thought that you cannot take your memories with you."

Peter King monitored the whole situation, watching Bobbi take one look at a textbook and the other at Eddie.

"The final things that you see," Eddie repeated.

Danielle Lynne could hear the rumbling down the hallway and woke very slowly to be reminded that Christmas vacation was over only to be replaced by a cold floor added with friends. Next sound the sophomore heard was the jingling of keys and the white light that appeared when the door opened when the blonde wearing the white uniform entered the room.

"Hello," Danielle Lynne picked her head up from the pillow.

"You up?" was the answer and the bright lights inside the room lit up immediately.

"Now, I am."

"Welcome back," Bobbi said, "your boyfriend is a trip."

"My what," Danielle Lynne remarked.

"We all had dinner at Denny's and I brought back some of my Grand Slam; you want some?"

Getting her coherence back, Danielle figured out what Bobbi meant by the 'boyfriend' comment and then realized there was a midnight snack inside the plastic container.

"Sure," and the nursing student handed the food over to her roommate and just watched Danielle Lynne put the fork to the leftovers.

"Eddie has seen a lot," Bobbi sat on the bed, "he told me one of his roommates died."

Danielle Lynne placed the empty tin on the chair that was by her desk, "I did not know he had a roommate here."

"No, when he was in the hospital."

"I heard something like that, it circulated around the barn that I was at doing juniors,"

"So you knew Eddie Patrick before meeting him at school?"

"I knew of him and our barn used to watch him develop therapeutic horseback riding."

"Therapeutic what?"

"It is how Eddie started riding with a leader of a two side-walkers and everything," Danielle Lynne divulged, knowing she did not have time trying to get points for her shot at the National Championship, "and now he is an independent rider getting ready to learn how to jump a fence."

Taking the Styrofoam plastic container from her, Bobbi remembered back to when they were registering a year ago and she spotted him making out his sheet which included a four hundred level class with the COM prefix. When she questioned him, he told her that his major was Communication and the nursing student was taken aback, wondering what he was going to do with that degree.

"With The Great Satan he can jump," Danielle Lynne told her roommate about her horse that she knew like the back of her hand, "he actually covers them when the two go over the fence."

One thing Eddie Patrick did well that Bobbi could remember was knowing his strengths and weaknesses. It was one of the things that impressed the blonde-haired caregiver about the fellow student who was always neatly dressed. Unlike Danielle Lynne inside the show ring where she worked in the proper dress, which included a pressed white shirt with a closed collar, a jacket, britches, and boots, Bobbi only started to wear the traditional whites in the fall after she completed the first year at Southern Dominican Catholic University as a volunteer at the hospital during the high school years where like Danielle Lynne the concept of giving care in a pink-striped outfit was seen as having the chance to wear the uniform. For Danielle Lynne it was the red jackets she saw up close up at Devon and Sussex when it was a big thing to gain points for her National Championship at those events when presenting respectful showings.

"She covers you?"

"Let's just say if I go left, he goes left."

"Right," Bobbi chuckled, slipping off her white shoes and collapsing on the bed.

"Only when I go right."

"Classes start tomorrow," Bobbi stated, shutting off the light above her head.

"That is funny," she continued after hearing what was said.

Tempting Time

Eddie Patrick was back in reality with his canes and the shorts that exposed the small incisions that were on his legs from childhood. Despite being in the classroom where the professor was lecturing about something where the information would only be useful in table conversation, the academic setting still acted like a security blanket.

Scribbling on the legal pad seemed to be an intelligent thing to do, and Eddie started to look forward to lunch and spending a relaxing night in the library.

"Are you heading up to the farm to practice?"

"No, Danielle Lynne's got the car."

Leaning back in his seat, Peter King kept listening to the monologue and once the class discussion of one finished the students made their way into the Florida sunshine.

"So, Danielle Lynne has the car and you are trapped on campus."

"Oh, I need to go to the library," was the reply from the fellow communication student.

As a friend, Peter checked his mental notebook and proceeded into the bright sunshine, making his way to the office in one of the other buildings. In a traditional fashion Eddie continued at his free spirit pace, heading to the cafeteria and grabbing both canes, he made it up the stairs to see Abigail sitting there reading a book.

Now on the second level, the canes went back to being supportive and he headed over to Abigail who still had her nose in the book.

"So, Abigail, how are you doing?"

"You can go up there, stand in line, and get the food then I will get your tray."

"Okay, Abigail."

Snickering, watching him gimp up to the line, she watched with great interest how he just accomplished all these things when she was lucky to read a chapter in a book.

After a few minutes, Eddie had the tray ready to go, and Abigail was right there in a friendly trusting fashion.

"Come on, gimpy, I have a few minutes to blow off."

Putting Together Facts to Determine a Fair Opinion

Peter King arrived in the newsroom after class and his 'part-time course credit getting financial aid' secretary left yellow sticking little square papers called "post its" all over the place. "Baseball try outs, basketball practice, and the fall sports banquet."

They all wanted pictures, Peter thought, *I should send Gimpy over to the banquet as a fall sport and his National Championship.*

Here was the journalistic debate for the college editor, Gimpy, like he pinned the nickname on him and rode in a competition with the name 'National' in the title. According to Gimpy, there were athletes from all over the country at this event. Once again according to Gimpy, he qualified under the National rules and attended the games where he won his division. Following proper collegiate logic academic theory, putting these facts not opinions together made him a national champion. Granted Southern Dominican Catholic University has not had a national champion except maybe the soccer team that had three exiled Cubans who ranged in age from 28–35 finishing medical school, the well-known academic school could use that title 'National Champion' in its school newspaper.

Picking up his camera, Peter exited the one-roomed office and headed down the dark hallway that was soon engulfed in sunshine in the main social hall.

"Peter," he heard the call.

"Thanks a lot for doing that story on me, my coach back home laughed so hard and really appreciated the call and my quotes," the senior wearing a SDCU baseball hat said.

Walking outside and looking up to the steeple that towered into the sky it was then he noted, in his mind, that the educational work he was doing filled the proper moral commitments that the school influenced the student within the thirteen months that he had resided on campus.

Schooling and Communicating Artistically

While Eddie was scribbling on his legal pad, Danielle Lynne communicated with The Great Satan in a way that seemed very trustworthy. Constantly, the two went at it when she moved around the dusty ring; The Great Satan pulled his head while she pulled back.

Due to school, Danielle Lynne had only made it out to the barn a few times and luckily Eddie was gracious enough to lend her the car to accomplish this workout.

The Great Satan pulled once again and she pulled back in a sarcastic way, giving the simple canter the vision of a tug-of-war contest. In this female versus male, female versus herself, female versus nature ultimate conflict the victor was going to determine the direction the pair was going. .

"Easy, you devil," she whispered to her friend, trying to keep him relaxed.

One of the barn rats put the rail at about three feet upon the rider's instructions and Danielle Lynne decided it was time to take the fence.

Applying pressure by using the inside of her leg was done with a sensitive kicking signal that explained to the large pony that it was time to move and , the two cantered past the stalls to the end of the ring. Continuing in the third gate, Danielle Lynne brought the rocking horse motion to a well-choreographed site when the two came together as they made a straight line to the fence. Despite the routine workout, Danielle Lynne could feel the tightness in her face and this only made her concentrate on the fence as she stared down in the center of the red mark.

Smoothly in her jumping position, Danielle Lynne was starting to enjoy the confident aura when The Great Satan brought his back feet down without a sound.

"Good Boy," she told her, putting both reigns in one hand to pat the shoulder, "good boy."

"That is enough for today," she heard Mr. Hawthorne shout from the grassy gallery of lawn chairs while his pipe seemed like a relaxing fixture on a perfect landscape.

A Nap Before Flap Jacks

Bobbi was taking her own message of structure when she vegged out on the bed inside her dorm room that barely fit one person.

"Abigail is starting to be a student," she chuckled, flipping her legs back on the floor after the fifteen minute power break.

Pulling the huge text out, she placed it on the desk and opening to the proper chapter the pages were decorated with yellow markings from her time in the library.

"I am so hungry," Danielle Lynne screamed when her tan pants showed hard work when entering into the dorm room.

Taking one more stare to the yellow markings that break was needed to be taken, she flipped back to her roommate.

"Chocolate Chip pancakes."

"Chocolate Chip pancakes?" Danielle Lynne questioned while she softly placed the keys to the car on the table.

"We can go down to the twenty-four diner and get some of the best chocolate chip pancakes."

Clasping the keys back to her riding pants' nylon belt holders, Danielle Lynne reminded her roommate that she had access to the car.

"Do you think he will mind?"

"No, let's go."

And the two headed down the hallway into the white lights from the street. Since the car was parked in the driveway that centered all the dorms, interacting with the guys was really simple, and coming from the library was Peter King with his photography equipment around the shoulder.

"Oh, you got Gimpy's car, where are you going?"

"To get some chocolate chip pancakes; do you want to come?" Bobbi Barnes invited him, not thinking to ask Danielle Lynne if it was all right to put another person in the car.

"Sure," was his answer and before the word was out of the mouth Peter was on the backseat while the girls were in the power positions up front.

"Where is Eddie?" Danielle Lynne requested.

"I do not know, I think he is still at the library."

A Black And White Day at the Races

In his stall, The Great Satan quietly chomped away in the grain bucket and came out to the light to see what was going on and there stood Angel Damian. Knowing this was not the time for feeding, he went back to the back of the stall and took another mouthful of feed. Coming back to the front, the chestnut belonging to Danielle Lynne, the college girl, watched intently as the groom took a few carrots out of her pocket to give to the other mounts that she was closest to.

"I miss you guys," she said and The Great Satan opened her ears a little more to hear everything.

"I miss you guys so much," the monologue continued, "like today I showed up to work and it was my time to head to the backstretch with a claimer, those are the ones who spend a lifetime living on the edge going from Motel 6 to Motel 6 always searching for a job not like you all who have fine saddles and elegant equipment."

"This morning it was like he was just coming out of a drunken state," she explained to the stable and they all had their eyes perked despite the late hour, "really trying but not really there."

"When I first got on him he seemed angry," Angel Damian continued, "it was like I was waking him up to do work at a time when he wanted just to stand there in his rental apartment."

Angel Damian clasped her hands and continued to tell the story about how the workday was going on in the backstretch at the local race track.

"So, we go to the entry on the track and Mr. Walt was there holding the stop watch and instructed me to do the workout at six furlong."

"So, I brought him to the gate and we sat in that metal contraption, waiting and waiting as the sun was rising."

Without even snorting, the stable listened and did not flinch, not even when the flies tried to interrupt the storytelling by Angel Damian.

"Then the doors opened and that is when she knew it was time to run," she reverted back to the little girl, talking about her first time over a fence, "and boy, did she run as fast as the wind and felt my body along for the ride."

As Angel Damian wrapped up the story, the horses continued to concentrate in an unobtrusive manner and it really made her feel welcome at the place that was a second home.

Since being a hot walker brought in some extra cash, she could afford personalized plates, feeling a little relieved from getting the stress that things were not going as clean like a hunter round. She opened the stall, not noticing the figure in the dark observing the action with a golden spark near his mouth.

Seeing the white, green, and orange plates with the letters "yin yang" on it, Nathaniel Hawthorne chuckled, knowing the test was being taken one conflict at a time.

The Rules Are the Rules

With one of those same yellow markers in his hand that Bobbi Barnes used to decorate her nursing text books, Eddie Patrick followed the lecture about black and white issues that needed to be handled by not challenging the waves, instead, by flowing calmly through the wake. As the intellectual studies started to be tiring sessions Eddie closed the black paperback with a grainy image strutting on the cover.

Herman Hesse, I wonder if he ever pumped gas, the young man with canes chuckled, smirked, knowing another period was complete and lunch was right across the campus. Closing the book which signaled ending the session for the day.

Since he had been going all morning, there was no need to worry about where his car disappeared too. And this coupled with the fact Danielle Lynne never showed her face before heading off to class, he gave the Jersey Girl perfect trust in his prize possession of independence.

While walking across campus, he heard a voice from the other side, "Mr. Patrick, Mr. Patrick, can I talk to you for a second?" It was a burly man wearing a security outfit that copycatted Miami Vice.

"Yes," Mr. Patrick replied to the academic watchdog.

"Mr. Patrick, your motor vehicle is parked illegally over by the nursing school, there is supposed to be no motor vehicles parked on the perfectly manicured lawns, the rules are the rules."

Putting two plus two together, Eddie Patrick figured his friends mistakenly dropped the car off. Talking his way through the conversation in gimpy ease, Eddie was able to get some time to find his keys.

As the security guard departed, he snickered, knowing the truth behind the illegal act committed by Southern Dominican Catholic University's only national champion.

Blowing off the quick fix eatery, Eddie made it back to the single room and when he came to the mat, found the locksmith's livelihood securely underneath the welcome message.

From the distance he heard someone in the vestibule mimic the words, "The rules are the rules."

"Peter," Eddie yelled back, putting the keys in his pocket.

Therapeutic Riding

As the horses on the backstretch chomped on the grain, Angel Damian glanced over her shoulder with a tray in her hands at the short blond-haired individual on crutches coming into the door.

"Well, look what the dog just brought in," one of the reporters covering the morning workouts barked when the leading jockey at the time of her spill entered into the food court designed for the workers close to the horses.

"You were going for some time, Miss Crawford?"

"And I still am in the hunt against these boys."

"Can we quote you on that?" they replied, pulling their early morning notebooks out with the scribble pencils.

"Do you all understand what you write in those things?"

Angel Damian started to chuckle, "Caroline Crawford out of the hospital after a weekend stay."

It was a claiming race; the fifth one on the card and her horse bolted from the starting gate and headed on the backstretch in fine fashion when all of a sudden the horse tripped, lost his balance and there was no chance to cover. Just like a rearing, it started in a flash and ended in the flash, and the next thing she saw upside down was her mount standing with her leg up.

"You poor thing," she remembered saying before dozing off on the dirt track.

On the dirt track, a human ambulance along with a horse van came onto the racing surface and Caroline never heard any of this as the unconscious lass took an unwanted nap.

Actually, the next thing she noticed was waking up with white lights in a daze as health care workers scurried around when her leg had a painful tingle. Fear gripped her at this time when they went to work finding out there were three .broken bones.

"Am I alive?" she whispered and a white uniformed individual smile.

"Yes, you are and you are going to be fine," the nurse remarked back, giving the patient reassurance that things were going to all right. This good news was received by someone who, only hours ago, was commanding a thousand pound animal down the stretch.

Grabbing an apple and joining Angel Damian at the cash register, Caroline smiled, pulling some change out of her pocket.

"Breakfast," the jockey told the hot walker brushing behind her like two horses battling the final furlongs to the finish line.

Beisbol to Futbol

Fluffing her hair, Abigail gave another look into the mirror while she twisted her golden 'A' into place. Putting the make-up on, giving one last application before game time, she grabbed the pompoms and headed out of the female locker room onto the cement driveway which led to the soccer fields.

Since Southern Dominican Catholic University never invested in a football team, it was up to Abigail and a couple friends to form the new cheerleading squad. Today it was a trial to cheer at a soccer game and as she crossed the driveway, the energetic enthusiast stopped in her tracks when Jake, or as Eddie would call him Jake The Jock, was in tight shorts, jogging with his long sleeve pitcher tee shirt showing his biceps that were a major eye appealing feature to the nearly twenty-year-old trying to make strides on campus.

She was in her second day on campus and the first person Abigail met that was the opposite sex was Jake promoting an athletically build. Their first conversation seemed very easy going with the fifteen minute interaction having no signs that anyone else was in the picture.

Continuing to the long field, she arrived where two other girls were sitting on the bench, waiting for their leader.

"Two four six eight, our captain Abigail is a little late," one said with a sophomoric grin.

Trying to keep a smile, knowing she took a little too long to doll up, the enthusiastic side line entertainer greeted her mates in traditional fashion.

"All right, I know I am a little late but this is just an experiment and whose results should be interesting."

"Yeah, Abigail, what's the point?" Another one asked, peering out to the strange sport that was not constructed for cheerleading like football, "Jake doesn't play this thing."

"Well, the sisters asked me to show support to other athletic sports not just…"

"Not just what?"

Logically Speaking

"Let me get this straight," the pigtailed blonde said in the back of the car with her equestrian friend, who was sitting there patiently, as they watched their mother deposit a check into the bank.

"Danielle Lynne is trying to be an Olympian equestrian," she started to assess the manner, "and Eddie is our national champion."

"Yes, at the walk."

"But a national champion nonetheless since he beat other competitors from other states."

"Right," her friend confirmed.

"Angel Damian no longer works at the ranch," Mischa Taylor continued to connect the dots together.

"No, yes, Angel Damian no longer works at the farm," Autumn Barton listened intently.

Looking at her checkbook and writing the balance into the small box, she noticed the two ten-year-olds in the backseat.

"Did you say Angel Damian left the barn?"

"That is right, Mrs. Taylor. Angel left the farm but no fret; Danielle Lynne is here now and she is going to be an Olympian in the Korean games."

"Really, and who told you that?" Mrs. Taylor questioned the youngster.

"Mr. Hawthorne when Miss Danielle Lynne arrived at the farm."

"Anyway, Mischa, what do you want to do this weekend?"

"Children's hunter."

Prepping for the Future

It was later in the morning and Caroline was on horseback with the assistance from her groom friend and Angel smiled, not realizing what to say after seeing the aggressive athlete back in the saddle. Despite mending a broken leg, the place to be first thing in the morning was working the starting gate with the maiden claimers.

"Look, kid, do not let the cast fool you, it was this or hobbling out here on crutches," she smirked at Angel Damian.

That is true, Angel Damian thought to herself, *it was quite a distance from the barn to the schooling gate.*

Taking the horse's lead line from the groom, Angel Damian walked the scared filly into the metal contraption and Caroline, from a distance, watched the fearful two-year- old animal trust the human beings as she was led into a box filled with bars that resembled prison gates.

Finding a metal ledge to stand on where the starters usually occupy during the race day, Angel Damian stroked the filly's face with a soft hand.

"Just let her stand there," she could hear Caroline command, "by the time this plaster thing is off my leg she will be looking forward to going into that cell and be wanting to get the high of jumping out of that when the bell goes off and seeing six furlongs to run with nothing in front of her."

"Easy, girl," Angel stared into the youngsters eyes and at that moment she saw the racing glare develop in the child's attitude which spelled out that this one was ready for business.

Grooming for the Future

"That is right, Miss Barton, it is three strides to the fence not four," Mr. Hawthorne laughed, putting the green hose back around the fence post.

Feeling a lump in her throat, Autumn sat back after the final fence in the small ring, knowing that the space between the next to last obstacle and the last on the course was in no way intended to be measured in four strides. If her pony did not have knowledge of going over fences, Autumn was going to have to count the four rhythms to figure out the problem.

Coming to a complete halt, she was able to relax and recount her thoughts like a youngster on verge of being a teenager.

"Good job, New Hope," she whispered into the gray mare's ear, knowing her horse covered the mistake.

"It is really nice when such a good pony takes care of things," Mr. Hawthorne reminded the rider in the ring that this activity was a humbling experience.

Feeling the sweat underneath her pre-junior, the rider loosened her arms and allowed New Hope to have his mouth back. Relaxing in a nice fashion, the junior high student smiled when they passed the rail where Mr. Hawthorne was finishing with the watering.

"We are going to beat Sebastian this week."

"So you will be showing this weekend?"

"Yeah, and I am going to beat Sebastian in the Children's Hunter Classic."

Mr. Hawthorne chuckled while returning to the barn, remembering when he was her age, wanting to outdo his neighbor on the baseball field. To say the least, Nate Hawthorne ended up succeeding in the other Doubleday sport dependent on leather equipment.

Ending up in the tack room, he pulled the saddle off the rack that only a few days ago magical potion was being applied to make Eddie's back straighter when sitting on The Great Satan.

"Yeah, every child should have a chance to succeed."

Staring at the leather seat, he could hear shouting from the washing area, "Mr. Hawthorne, should I put New Hope in the field or stall?"

"Put him the field."

Making sure everything was dried, she fastened the nylon lead line and walked New Hope to the gate where there was green grass everywhere. New Hope acted cordially like the good friend knowing that his trusted partner was looking out for the best for his accomplice in equine education.

Mr. Hawthorne watched the child polish off the work that adults do in the same manner and to top it off, after New Hope was let loose, Autumn pulled a carrot from her back pocket and shared it with the horse.

"It is a good day," Mr. Hawthorne noted in his mind.

Paying for a Label

Bobbi Barnes crumpled the dry cleaning bill in her hand, knowing the cost was starting to be a burden to the college student. Unlike the baseball team that Abigail hung out with, the cost to keep her look in professional manner had an expense account that rivaled the books at the store.

Driving the car into the parking lot, she navigated the way through while a song played on the radio despite the student not knowing what was exactly being talked about in the ballad.

Pulling into a space by her dorm, she collected the books she had on the passenger seat and headed past the pool where Abigail was sitting reading a book that was not a text instead, it was a classic that used to be tested on in high school.

"What are you doing?" Bobbi questioned, unlatching the gate.

Still in a comfortable outfit from attending class, Abigail looked up from the small paperback, "I am reading *The Scarlet Letter*."

"What's next; you are going to finally hand in the paper that was due two years ago?"

"No, it is just an interesting story."

"I thought you hated it."

"Well, that was when there was a test on every chapter."

"And you were more interesting in cheerleading practice?"

"No, also that 'A' label thing now seems to have a different meaning to it."

"How so?"

"Granted Abigail committed adultery but what does happen when you have one or more guy friends?"

"But that was not what Abigail was like?"

"Well, in high school you meet a guy or you get google lee eyed with him and that is the only guy you know."

"Yeah."

"Back then they did not pick up and go to college."

"Oh, you meet other people when you go to college," Bobbi finally figured she got something through Abigail's mind, "something more than Mr. Notre Dame."

Both of them chuckled as the nursing student enjoyed the late afternoon Florida sun.

"Abigail wore an 'A' and Eddie has canes," Bobbi heard her say with eyes shut.

"Hmm," was the health care worker's response.

Spending Time Off

Danielle Lynne, the equestrian looking for direction while thinking it was in the competitive exhibition ring, sat on the wooden chair in the dorm room that was carpeted through a sharing relationship with her roommate.

On the television, the bunny ears distributed an image of a young gymnast dressed in pink leotards stand over a bin filled with white chalk.

"Nice Saturday afternoon of work," Bobbi stormed into the room and announced.

"I am just sitting here watching the sports spectacular," Danielle Lynne confessed, "it's women's gymnastics, they look twelve, and what is it."

"Well, they do have a horse in it?" the student nurse showed her athletic education, "don't they?"

"Yes, Bobbi, they have a horse in gymnastics, ha ha, and they have leather in baseball while figure skaters do basic dressage moves," she watched the perfect body run to the apparatus and miss her mark.

"Do I smell an ounce of resentment?"

"Ow, that must have hurt," Danielle Lynne blurted out.

"What happened?" the nurse watched the young girl start to cry.

"She blew it."

"Well, she will probably cut a television deal and be a superhero or something, I wouldn't worry about it," the health care worker verbally gave a prescription.

"You're right, they are on stage," Danielle Lynne defended her activity with exhibitors that considered itself as a sport, "we do not have to be on stage, just proudly display our colorful affordable dollar ribbons that rival their million dollar sponsor contract and we looked just as good on national television at the 84 games as Miss Smiley Face."

Snickering about the priorities of the dedicated and committed, the health care worker flopped on the bed in the same way she did on the lounge chair by the pool, "It's Saturday night, we should go out."

"I actually have a meeting with Eddie, at four in the morning," Danielle Lynne reported "we set a time for breakfast to get together before heading to the horse show to school, the kids."

"You're right, I need to get sleep and I really should be rested to head to the library."

"But next week?" Bobbi finished the sentence.

"Yes, next week."

Getting Ready to School

It was very early in the morning, or very late at night, as Eddie paid the bill at the 24-hour restaurant and a now perky Danielle Lynne had the cup of coffee to go in her well-manicured hands.

Bustling in were a couple Southern Dominican Catholic University students coming back from walking the strip all night. Danielle Lynne was ready to offer them some of her java but pulled back, knowing it was going to be the final minutes of peace until they pull the car back into the university parking lot.

Due to the hour, the freeway was empty going north bound but the two looked over to the southbound side which had a nice congestion heading back from the legendary spring break Mecca called Fort Lauderdale.

When the duo arrived at the exit saying Fort Lauderdale with the arrows to the beach pointing right, their car made the left heading west inland getting closer to the Gator Glades State Park. Right before the Florida's Death Valley rural stretch of road started without any rest stops, the preserved land was situated for all the residents to escape to when things were getting too cosmopolitan. Eddie guided his car with ease through the construction zone that opened up and making a quick turn they found themselves at the farm.

Already there was plenty of emotion down at the barn that lacked Angel Damian's managerial skills, and it seemed to be running smoothly when a very dedicated Autumn Barton took the situation seriously when her competitive edge took over when 'New Hope' was going to give Sebastian a run for his money.

Stepping out and stretching her legs, Danielle Lynne raised her arms which woke Eddie up watching the white shirt worn his friend Looking back at the steering wheel, the wrist bands brought him back to reality while his riding partner started down to the commitment like going to Church on Sunday.

"Danielle Lynne," Mr. Hawthorne could be heard down in the manila white light that had the darkness as a backdrop, "we need help to hook up the trailer."

"New Hope, stop," echoed like a stereo sound to the rider's right.

With two canes in hand, Eddie slowly made it down to the area where all the commotion was stirring, "Eddie, you will be on The Great Satan today in a couple flat classes."

143

Turning around, Danielle Lynne smiled, "This is it, don't worry, let's have fun with it."

Already prepared in his athletic uniform—the tan britches and white tee shirt—he knew that this was something he wanted to do for a long time. Competing in a regular horse show with a barn that supported each other was a very comfortable feeling for someone who was looking for an accomplishment.

"Now, Autumn, is New Hope giving you a hard time?"

"I think he did not like to be woken up this early in the morning," the ten-year-old retorted.

"Well, it is time for everybody to wake up and do their best."

Over the next few minutes, Eddie made his way into the tack room where the early morning air seemed to hold the innocence to the new day. Giving a quiet yawn, he double checked his trunk to see that all the equipment was together and ready to be shipped the quarter mile to the show grounds.

"Danielle Lynne, my trunk is ready to go."

No longer having a college student look, Danielle Lynne popped her head into the tack room door.

"Why don't you get in the truck?"

Seeing the trailer with The Great Satan and New Hope both securely fastened in the trailer, Eddie knew it was time to enjoy this moment.

Resting in Peace

When Bobbi turned over to look above her pillow, she was used to the fact that Danielle Lynne had her spread down while the bed was empty. It hit her in a strange way this time that she was off campus already and her clock only read seven.

Flipping her legs onto the cold floor, the nursing student stood up, coming to closure that the benefit to being alone in the room was there was nobody in the way to use the shower. Taking one more glance at the door, she noticed it was not locked and walking over she flipped the latch, making sure her environment was secure.

"Oh geez, she just ran out of here," Bobbi said, half asleep and returning to the only other piece of furniture in the room that was considered hers and fiddled with the pages to the text book.

The clock now read 7:03 in the morning and it was still another three hours until the only mass during the day at the chapel.

Taking another hard stare at the textbook, Bobbi Barnes closed it then sat back down on the bed, contemplating that it was Sunday morning and this was how the day was supposed to be spent.

Arriving at School

Jessica McCord was on Sebastian in the schooling ring when the trailer with The Great Satan and New Hope drove up to the grounds where they were slated to perform.

With a bagel and cream cheese in her tiny hands, she clucked with one hand on the reigns. Knowing Jessica was still having breakfast, Sebastian slowly plodded to the gate to watch The Great Satan and New Hope get off the moveable stall.

Keeping his cool, Sebastian heard everything Jessica whispered while finishing the bread donut. It was not the fact she was being an elitist; instead, here were two friends from two different barns at an activity where only parents and friends attend for the sole reason of spending a Sunday doing something productive.

Granted, around Christmas time the youngsters all dressed up to attend a formal party down by the ocean on the Fort Lauderdale strip where awards were handed out confirming 'job well done' after they ate roast beef garnished with mashed potatoes. And to close the evening, the grand champion was announced, giving credibility for doing all this at such an early hour.

Sebastian just watched New Hope step off the ramp and the little girl, who was as large as Jessica, take control of the situation by inserting the metal hook on to the nylon halter.

"C'mon, New Hope," she told her best friend, noticing Jessica and Sebastian already schooling in the ring, "we are not late, they are just going to get tired and dirty earlier."

As the final bite to the bagel went into Jessica's mouth, she pulled up the reigns and quickly broke into the canter, making a big circle then plopping over the two fences that were an 'X' in the middle of the ring.

"Show off," Autumn mumbled seeing Jessica's perfect position when going over the obstacle.

Opening Prayer

"Show off," Abigail the cheerleader chuckled with hands clasped and on her knees in the pew.

"What, I am opening the meeting with God and Jesus."

"Opening the meeting with God and Jesus?"

"Yes," Bobbi responded, leaning back on the pew seating section while Abigail went into her relaxing state, "Actually, we are supposed to be straighter until Father Roger comes down the aisle."

"Actually, I had a bad night last night."

"I worked yesterday, what did you do?"

"Okay, I worked out last night."

Father Lloyd then came down the aisle and the two girls watched him in the color of the season make his way to the pulpit. Now standing, the pair felt something in the Southern Dominican Catholic University air that the Sisters who ran the campus called the Holy Spirit. After the opening prayer, the girls sat down and were engulfed in a thought process that only they knew was possible.

Take Five

Danielle Lynne dismounted The Great Satan and unhooked the blue jacket, exposing the elegant white riding shirt. Turning to Uncle Nathan, she smiled, "Uncle Nate, it was a nice round."

"Sure was," he responded, "now get Eddie up, you got the step ladder, right?"

Since Danielle Lynne went early in the round, they had plenty of time to exchange riders, and the pre junior groom was standing there with the ladder for Eddie to use it like a mounting ramp. As the ten-year-old steadied the three step blue wooden apparatus, Danielle Lynne assisted Eddie putting his leg in one stirrup then throwing the other one across so he was sitting straight in the brown leather tack used as a seat.

First thing Danielle Lynne noticed was how straight Eddie's back was when the two walked in to be judged. "Eddie looks very powerful up there," she interpreted to Uncle Nate.

"I put the magical spray on the saddle."

"You did not," Danielle Lynne chuckled like a niece at a family get together, "you are not still putting magical spray on saddles to help kids sit up straight in the saddle?"

"Sure, I am."

A pin drop could be heard as the silence was only interrupted when the announcer broke in with the command for what the riders needed to do next. In the first direction, Danielle Lynne seemed very optimistic as Eddie held his own inside the schooling show ring.

Then it happened when they changed direction and were asked for the trot, "Ah, shoot, Eddie, you're on the wrong diagonal," Danielle Lynne winced.

"It's his outside leg, it was not strong enough to keep up."

For the rest of the class, Danielle Lynne concentrated on that outside leg, wondering how he could make it stay up with the up and down motion during the trot.

Smiling, Mr. Hawthorne saw the honest college attitude in Danielle Lynne's eyes, knowing that those logical decisions in her head were spinning as she watched something that naturally unfold.

"Okay, Danielle Lynne," Mr. Hawthorne started to teach, "why do you think Eddie lost the diagonal over there in the corner?"

"His outside is his right side and when he walks it is usually stronger on the left," Danielle Lynne responded.

"You noticed?"

"Yes, Uncle Nate, I noticed," she smiled, "but I do not really think it was his disability or weak leg that knocked him off the diagonal."

"Hmm."

Danielle Lynne walked over to the in gate as Eddie Patrick came over with the fifth place ribbon in his hand.

"Well, there were five in the class."

"And what a nice color for your dorm room," Danielle Lynne suggested, taking the bridle in her hand, assisting Eddie out of the ring.

Putting on a Good Show

It was now her home and with the leather halter over the shoulder, Angel Damian made it into the rail bird cove. Trying not to slip on the traditional litter that lined the grandstand floor, the future jockette found a spot and pulled out the white piece of paper with the word 'show' printed on the slip.

All of a sudden, a bell rang and the horses exploded from the gate and the groom/hot walker saw the barns colors from a distance where binoculars were needed to see the action up close. Knowing Caroline had her mount under control, the runners disappeared behind the scoreboard announcing all the odds. Depending now on the call, Angel Damian kept her eye focused when it appeared as a pack of brownish mass behind a wall of trees.

Caroline was in contention, ready to make a move and Angel Damian kept staring at the number five.

Within seconds, the group came to the head of the stretch and the crowd got up and roared, no longer were the beer bottles the main activity to the day; instead, the challenge of reading newspaper statistics followed by deciding who was going to win the race held priority as the truth was revealed on the track.

Angel Damian could definitely see Caroline do her sixty to ninety second job as they thundered to the finish.

Once they crossed the line, Angel Damian removed the halter, noting the number five from her relaxed position and hooked the lead line to the circular metal piece. Flipping the latch open, her brown-booted stable shoes hit the dirt and she suddenly heard someone behind her mention.

"Excuse me, sweetie," the person holding a big camera said, "coming through."

Stepping forward, Angel Damian met the four-legged animal with the matching number on the halter.

"I hope you did not lose your lunch money on that one," Caroline stated from above.

"Nah, had it to show."

"Had it to show?" Caroline quickly asked while popping off the mount then disappearing through the archway.

Whispering with the horse whose attention now focused on a new leader, "Yeah, had it to show."

By the hour the races were over, Angel Damian finished off the final stall and headed back over into the grandstand.

Finding a teller that was still open, she handed the piece of paper to the clerk who inserted it into the machine.

"$2.20," he said without even a comment.

Putting the two dollars back into her wallet, Angel Damian suddenly found herself by the fountain that graced the paddock area. Taking one of the nickels she flung it into the water and closing her eyes.

"Yeah, it was for show."

A School Ring

For the past three minutes, Autumn was concentrating on the children's hunter course taking two foot fences like it was a grammar test. Counting strides in New Hope's ear, the two flawlessly flew over each obstacle in a way that would make a painter put a brush to a canvas.

Finally, she completed the eight obstacle course featuring only four fences, tired, she pulled up and looked around to catch Mr. Hawthorne smile while clapping his hands.

Taking a deep breath, she halted the horse only to cluck again to do the four fence eight obstacle course a second time, "That was good New Hope and this one is to beat Sebastian," she lip synched so the judge would not hear the communication between friends.

Danielle Lynne had finished putting the gookety gook, as she liked to call it, on her saddle and joined Uncle Nate at the rail as New Hope did his duty by taking each question, forcing his rider to think their way through the situation.

"Boy, is she looking good," the experienced college student remarked.

"Yes, she is," Nathaniel Hawthorne replied, watching his client whose book bag in the truck was filled with colorful pictures of Christopher Columbus commanding the Nina, Pinta, and Santa Maria.

Coming to the second fence in the fourth line, the youngster perfectly did everything she was told to do and had a beautiful smile when putting the finishing touches on the round.

"I am going to beat Sebastian," she said as Mr. Hawthorne repeated the clapping applause, "That was a classic one Autumn, a classic one."

"Autumn Classic," Danielle Lynne deemed the rider met her mother at the gate ready with a bottle of water, "well, Autumn Classic, that was very nice."

"I am going to beat Sebastian, Mom," she squeaked, taking the spring water.

Ten minutes passed when all the riders that were reminiscent of a fourth grade recess returned to the ring for the flat class. There were five equestrians dressed in adult clothes and all wearing their hair in pigtails. In less than a day, they would all be on the playground representing different grades and discussing their horses, but for the next few moments there would be dead silence as the champion to the division would be crowned.

As they lined up to walk in a straight line, the dust kicked up which made Danielle Lynne sneeze, "Sit straight in the saddle," she coughed and the student all of a sudden stuck out her chest, making sure her back was in the proper place.

Dress shirt out of his pants and covered with red sweat dust, Eddie Patrick had his iced tea and bag of chips while watching the conclusion to the Autumn Taylor episode to the day's events.

She easily went into the first gait called a trot and just like the other ten-year-old peers, the elders noticed the grammar school fluent motion while going through the simple tasks that are taking for granted in the show ring when doing flat work.

There was no resentment being a spectator at the child's activity, only a warm feeling that he was supporting another barn member.

Both Danielle Lynne and Mr. Hawthorne watched everybody do a tear drop turn and go in the other direction after completing a canter.

"New Hope is such a good pony," Danielle Lynne mentioned to her Uncle.

"That she is."

Then it happened; after patting New Hope for doing a nice transition in the other direction, she was not able to get off on the right diagonal.

"Autumn," Danielle Lynne quietly squealed.

As the children's hunter over fences rider doing the flat work picked up that there was a mistake Autumn could hear in her mind the word 'shoot' she tried her best not to bring attention to the problem before fixing it.

"Autumn, when you make a mistake you quietly correct it," Danielle Lynne finished her sentence to herself, "drawing attention to yourself is circus like."

Stretching her hand to the outside by pulling it toward the rail, New Hope responded by going into a faster gait. Keeping her heels down and her chest out, she started to feel the strength of being in control.

With a lap around the ring complete, the announcer asked them to come back to a walk and stand in the center of the ring. Finding herself feeling confident, she never stopped sticking her chest out while coming into the ring getting ready to hear who won the class.

After the judge came into the ring followed by walking up and down the line like a General expecting the troops, she took out the walkie-talkie.

Then they told the public who won the class that did not involve Sebastian or New Hope. But when third place was called, Autumn broke out in a big smile when she left the ring.

"Third place," she told Danielle Lynne who took the reins, "I still beat Sebastian in all three classes but someone else won the division."

"That is all right," Danielle Lynne comforted, "but green, yellow, and red look really cool on the wall in the bedroom."

"I guess you're right, Miss Danielle Lynne."

Mr. Hawthorne had inserted the pipe into his mouth and smirked at Danielle Lynne, "A second, third, and fourth, nice work, Miss Danielle Lynne."

A Sunday Drive

Mass was ended and the two friends left in peace, ready to return to the books.

"So, what are you going to do the rest of the day?" Abigail asked, hitting the warm sun light.

"Hit the books."

"You worked all day yesterday and now you are hitting the books," Abigail questioned, standing in the comfortable rays.

"Yup."

"I have a Rick Springfield cassette in my car tape deck and I think I am going down to Collins Avenue and do the Hotel thing,"

"The Hotel thing,"

"Yeah, the Hotel thing."

Minutes later, as the Priest returned into the Chapel, Abigail took off to cruise Collins, while Bobbi walked across the driveway to the conveniently located library.

Sitting in the right car that her parents bought to celebrate finishing high school, the four wheels acted like a springboard to meet the right man. Putting the car into reverse, she headed off campus onto the open roadways that featured a sauna like excursion through traffic lights. As the foreign language store fronts passed by, the brunette with the cheerleader smile listened to the music on the radio until the causeway was just ahead and ready to be crossed.

Once the highway started to incline, Abigail's perfectly manicured nails pushed the car-friendly album into the tape deck.

Working Weekend Winding Down

With orange signs lining State Road 84, Angel Damian took her time in the dark as the dirt filled groom headed home from the backstretch. Hitting every light was not the intention and, boy, did she yearn for the expressway that the newspapers reported was the South Florida of the future.

Finally getting a break, she cruised through the intersection and the Sunday night seemed not to be the same until she came to County Line Boulevard. Making the left, she saw the red parking lights to the trailer and one little munchkin just trying to keep her best friend still while hosing him down.

"New Hope, stay still," Autumn Taylor requested as her horse's back legs took two steps in both directions, "stay still."

"Autumn, when you are done we have the third stall ready for you, but you may want to walk New Hope around the ring one time to let him dry off."

"Oh! My mother is not going to like having to wait, so, New Hope, you better dry off real quick."

Danielle Lynne came out of the stall that was reserved for New Hope and snuck into the tack room where Eddie Patrick was sitting quietly with his saddle.

"Hay."

"Hey."

In one smooth motion, she threw up the pad on to the saddle rack and turned around to the door.

"Hey."

"Hay."

Before Danielle Lynne could leave the enclosure, a voice came from the saddle rack.

"What did you think of my class today?"

"Well, the cantering was really nice; you were straight and that rocking chair motion suited you real well."

"Be honest, was it the rubber boots?"

"No, this was a schooling show so the rubber boots did not have anything to do with it," Danielle Lynne blurted out while thinking to herself, *"You lost the diagonal at the trot, then you got it back, then lost it, but you ended up on the right one in the end."*

When Autumn came around the bend, Danielle Lynne disappeared from Eddie's sight only to be heard by the children's rider.

"He looks tired," the college student commented.

"Yeah, I know, that is why I am putting him to bed," Danielle Lynne smiled, seeing the youthful innocence. "You know what, Miss Danielle Lynne?" the apprentice continued.

"What?"

"New Hope and I had a meeting while walking and he told me when I am on the wrong diagonal he is going to give me a secret sign to tell me to switch."

"Oh, Autumn, that is a good idea but make sure the judge does not see you two passing notes or—"

"Or what, Miss Danielle Lynne, the judge will change my seat," Autumn came to conclusion.

When Angel Damian saw the light turn green, she only had a few feet to drive until her living dwelling was in sight on the beach. It really wasn't a trailer park in the traditional sense of the word, instead, luxury affordable given to her as gratitude for supplying talent to an owner who needed the performance.

Pulling into the parking space on the grass, Angel Damian grabbed her overnight bag and found the keys, knowing it was going to be a nice day off tomorrow.

Sunday Night Silence

Abigail sat in the quad outside the theater where there once was a ghost who burned to death back when the university was a college exclusively for girls. Theater was not Abigail's thing; instead, her personality rivaled the obsession that strict book memorization entailed to properly perform on the lonely stage located behind her back.

Abigail thoughts were just like Eddie's when the Communication arts sophomore cleared his mind while cleaning his saddle. This quiet outdoor relaxing exercise was a Sunday evening task in which kept her calm between studies.

Standing up and brushing off her jeans was the next movement she made, deciding to leave the grassy location that was a nice place to meditate.

Crossing past the chapel and up the stairs, her independent beauty made her feel strong. Checking her watch and seeing the time, she remembered that cutting through the student hall was not an option.

"So, Eddie, why did you cut to the other line?" Danielle Lynne softly spoke while sitting on the couch.

"I do not take the bread from anyone besides the priest."

Settling back in the comfortable non-pew seating, Danielle Lynne smiled, knowing that this Eddie Patrick person at her barn takes thing seriously while he was very honest.

Once the mass ended and the small contingent were told to go in peace, she stood up.

"Time for the cookies."

Acting like a school girl slash Girl Scout, "I wonder if they have short bread cookies."

"They do."

"Cool."

Bypassing the holy activity that the cheerleader already experienced earlier in the day, Abigail kept her books to her heart as she trekked outside toward the dorm rooms.

Fast Food Thinking

As the fast food light gleamed into the car, Mrs. Barton gave a motherly look into her daughters eyes asked the question.

"So, how did Mischa Taylor do today at the horse show?"

"She did not show."

"Why didn't she show?"

"Her brother was in Daytona with his sports car."

"Oh."

"Eddie Patrick showed."

"Who's Eddie Patrick, darling?" her mother questioned while Autumn played with the French fries, "oh yeah, the handicapped rider."

"He's a college student with Miss Danielle Lynne, Mom," Autumn defended him, "and he did very well at the horse show except for one thing."

Starting to laugh at Autumn's small skeleton, "He lost his diagonal like I did."

"What do you mean diagonal?" Mrs. Taylor played dumb to make sure Autumn knew what she was doing.

"Mother," Autumn started, taking another bite to the burger, "when you are trotting."

"Now, Autumn, what is a trot?"

Sounding like an adult and not a fourth grader, Autumn explained in her own words that a trot was the second gait to a horse's movement. In the same way a person jogs, a horse moves a little faster when trotting.

"So, when you are trotting, the rider is supposed to rise in the seat when the outside leg moves forward."

"Why is that?"

"I do not know and please, Mom, stop complicating things," Autumn giggled, "anyway, Eddie 'Mr. National Champion at the walk' was not able to keep up with the outside leg."

"So, Autumn, what happens if you think you are on the wrong diagonal?"

Looking straight into the air, Autumn clearly repeated what Mr. Hawthorne said during a lesson, "You sit down and come back up when the outer leg goes forward."

"Hmm, that is interesting," Mrs. Barton answered, "oh, by the way, are you finished."

Having to think about it, Autumn sweated for a fraction of a second before saying, "I did my homework last night."

"I meant with the sandwich, silly," Mrs. Barton laughed before turning the ignition on and pulling the car in reverse.

Tempting The Great Satan and *Les Autres* (The Others)

Mr. Hawthorne opened each bill with his eyeglasses on his nose and knowing it was a month where Peter paid Paul. Checks arrived then were deposited and with the calculator's assistance, everything in the end came out to a zero balance. It was something Nathaniel Hawthorne did very well, not make commitments that he could not keep. It was the fall and he was not loading horses in Harrisburg to drive all the way to Washington DC then on to New York City. Instead, it was the local shows and the big moments happened when the kids did very well at an annual big show, followed by getting out of the equestrians outfits to transition into formal wear for the end of the year awards dinner where memorable moments were granted.

Mixed up in the stack was an envelope from a local organization that was hoping to help the special riders at County Line Stables. That is how Eddie Patrick found the farm during the first few months of his freshmen year. Despite the supportive community that made Southern Dominican Catholic University a major lure to higher education, the school did have a commuter enrollment which meant the weekends seemed pretty quiet.

Mr. Hawthorne could remember how he described where his sister ran away to so long ago. "Saturday Night was a graveyard," he said on top of a white gelding the first time at the stable. One thing the Eddie's trainer noted was that the single visit that turned into two to three and this year the whole weekend was he started to develop structure on campus. That meant having a schedule, forcing him to budget time between studies, and socialization where the communication skills are put into place. Just heading back to the dorm room only to sleep the afternoon away and heading to the library may be the rule of thumb at an Ivy League institution, but that does not create healthy quality thinking; instead, having goals outside the books allows the student to focus their attention on the task at hand.

Opening the letter, there was a very nice inquiry with a major donation opportunity through an auction geared toward memorabilia including a dress worn by a beauty queen who was caught in a political tryst. Laughing really hard about the incident that happened on a Miami yacht, Mr. Hawthorne decided to respond positively to the charities good will idea.

Counting Strides

Danielle Lynne found herself sitting next to reality as she took an Introductory to Psychology class, trying to decide if a horse's mind was different from a human. In the same way she studied a horse show prize list with an intended goal of what to compete over the weekend, Danielle Lynne made some objective decisions concerning the academics.

"What was a major?" the sophomore who was supposed to know everything pondered when the semester syllabus was passed out by the professor.

It seemed like the major was a commitment to something that they were really interested in studying and were in theory a strong point in a late adolescents thought process.

When finished distributing the outline to the winter/spring months, the professor turned around to explain to the roomful of people.

"This is not Screw With Your Mind 101, it is Introductory to Psychology," Danielle Lynne put the pen to the paper and thought through her training schedule, "if you make it to May and finish the assignments with passing grades you will be one small step in a very interesting journey into a very thought provoking science," Professor Sister McCoombs continued at the blackboard.

Still, Danielle Lynne jotted down some dates on the dates that were given to her to have different papers done and when to be prepared for tests.

"If this is an elective and you will never touch another psych issue in your academic life, the skills obtained during the time spent giving attention to this information could, and I stress, could assist in your daily life to deal with situation."

When Sister McCoombs was done lecturing, the information Danielle Lynne had already had the strategy how she was going to deal with the fences on this course.

Objective Observations

"Opinion," Professor Corman said.

Peter King yawned as did Eddie Patrick when the professor continued to talk in front of the class.

"Opinion and Fact."

"You know, Eddie, if you know the difference between opinion and fact studies say that you are a journalist."

"Now, Peter," Eddie whispered back, "do you think the study is an opinion or fact?"

"You got a point there."

Putting Letters to the Number of Years

"Well, well, nurses, in one more semester you are going to be Licensed Practical Nurses," Professor Lee Anne said.

"I get to have a name badge with my name and the letters LPN," Bobbi Barnes contemplated while doodling on the syllabus.

"It is not the letters LPN that matter right now," Bobbi Barnes looked up, "it is the skills you will learn to be a better person and at this stage of your college career a good mother."

Mouthing the word 'nurse', Bobbi Barnes was quickly corrected, 'caring person'.

A caring person was an interesting term, observed Bobbi, flipping through the five hundred page text that at the bookstore cost nearly thirty dollars and that did not reach the amount of time that was needed to decipher information in its contents.

"What was that?" Bobbi continued to play with the two words 'caring person' on her one sheet paper that contained her schedule for the next couple months.

Chapter II: Objective Observations

"Observe," Professor Corman said.

Peter King once again yawned, followed by a repeat performance by Eddie Patrick.

"And looking at something," the professor continued to lecture.

"Did you know studies say that you can look at something but not observe it?" Peter King whispered back to Eddie Patrick.

"Did you look at the study or observe the study?"

"I read it in the paper," Peter answered the question.

"Then you did not observe or look at the study instead, you read an opinion about facts in a study."

"Which could be viewed as developing our own opinions on something we read," Peter deducted.

"Or looked at in the newspaper," Eddie agreed.

"Or observed."

"True."

Ending their conversation, they both looked up at the Professor, who heard their whole conversation and did not stop them.

"Do you think we observed this lecture?" Peter asked his staff member.

"And developed opinions on what he said."

"That is it for today," Professor Corman stopped and smiled, knowing someone got something out of the platform he presented to the group of students in the year where they know it all but really do not know anything about reality.

Chapter III: Objective Observations

Wearing the Southern Dominican Catholic University cheerleading outfit with pride, Abigail popped to the top of the steps, flashing her meal ticket that doubled as identification to the old lady with a clicker. After grabbing some fruit and juice, she saw the group sitting at a table that featured Bobbi already out with the legal pad, jotting notes from the chapter that had small print despite its size.

"You know, I just watched these three kids play today at a kinder gym place across town,"

"Did you observe the children?" Eddie inquired.

"Or did you just look at the children?"

"I watched them," Abigail repeated.

"Why did you watch children at the kinder gym place across town?" Bobbi Barnes never even left her text to ask the question.

"I had an eight in the morning class and the syllabus said to go down to a kinder gym to watch the children for a half hour."

"Did you take notes?" Eddie continued the friendly interrogation.

"No."

"Pete, does that mean she observed or looked at the children?"

"I said I watched them," Abigail interrupted them restating her position, "I did not take notes so I was not observing them and it was not just a quick glance or a passive view, I watched them."

Starting to chuckle, Bobbi could not believe Abigail was developing conclusions and building concrete opinions through observing facts.

"So, is there a game tonight?" Bobbi pried.

"Yeah."

"So that brings up another question," Eddie continued the friendly exchange, "did the children watch, look, or observe you in a cheerleading outfit?"

Elective Official

After lunch, the trained caring person opened her dorm room to find Danielle Lynne lying on her bed with shoes off and the socks that she wore to class in the morning.

167

"I have to get to class," she said about her duties on the non-stable day, "and then I have one of those marathons at night."

"Which is?"

"Three hours of Mayan Geography and Ancient Asian Cultures."

"Three hours of what?" Bobbi gave a quizzical look at the roommate who was very strategic in thinking about her class plan.

"Mayan Geography and Ancient Asian Cultures," Danielle Lynne repeated, reading the paper back text book that cost her five bucks and change at the book store.

"That must be fun."

"It was an elective that fit my schedule and I have from Thursday at noon to Monday Morning to—"

"Study Mayan Geography and Ancient Asian Cultures."

Putting her shoes on, she grabbed the book for the one o'clock class, "No, to get to the barn so I can make it to Seoul in '88."

"Oh."

Show-Riding or Riding to Show

It was two men holding a stop watch, Angel Damian taking a seat in the grand stand still dealing with what happened in class today. Once again another claimer which only the daily chart readers would pick up on while 'studying', the races gave the goal-oriented high school dropout a little spat in the morning. Mr. Walt's friend, who was timing the exercise ride, looked at the handheld piece to see that the three-year-old just wasn't moving fast enough.

"Angel Damian," Mr. Walt called her over to the area where the pictures were snapped when the winner finished first, "that ride will get your number there," he said pointing to the trash can.

"Not there," changing his finger to the Winner's Circle.

Starting to judge the racing roadies, this Motel 6 reservation might find itself coming down in the thick of it giving all and sometime hit the top spot on the board with nice odds.

But the horse will be in the hunt down the stretch, milking the tote board in the five to six area, Angel Damian thought while watching the flickering lights to the odds for the opening maiden.

An hour later, standing up and turning away from the South Beach Downs infield flirting with the pond water, she walked through the Grandstand and noticed all the colorful silks that lined the plant. Just like the jumper course, the colorful atmosphere was appealing to the true youngster playing a game with adults who were known for their business sense.

Checks and Balances

Walking out of the house into the South Florida evening air, Mr. Hawthorne could hear the horses who were allowed to go out for the night. Carrying a bowl with apples, the trainer went over to the two monkeys who had lifetime living quarters right by the gate. Jeb and George were their names and they watched everybody come down to the stables then leave with great interest, wondering they would be a success in whatever endeavor they wanted. Despite their confinement, the two kept a close eye on the action, knowing that they had a great grasp on what was going on down at the barn.

For the past couple months, it had been interesting to see the regular barn manager leave to follow some dream of being a jockey and then there was the national champion who was crowned in the walk division of a disabled horse show. But, horses let that disabled word go by the wayside, since they even have to use all fours to balance themselves when going from point A to point B.

Then there was the Olympian or the person who had the dreams to go to the international games developed as peaceful relations between different countries in the horse-back riding division better known as the Equestrian with a more specific section called show jumping.

"Here, how are you two doing tonight?" he said, handing one apple to Jeb and the other to George.

Stripping the redness out of the fruit, Jeb enjoyed his snack while George let out a shriek.

In the moonlight, The Great Satan, who was the odd pony out, found himself roaming through a field of equine tossed salad.

"So, what do you two think about The Great Satan?" Mr. Hawthorne asked the two.

When no response meant, 'No comment', Mister Hawthorne continued walking to the gate as the lone white light shined on the rings on which the kids learned how to ride a horse unlike at other barns that had not only indoor rings but brightness that allowed students the opportunity to work on their skills after dark. But Mr.

Hawthorne believed in innocence and just like Wrigley Field, games were supposed to be played during the day.

With a steady gait, Mr. Hawthorne checked each stall and noticed that nothing was unusual as he continued through the open air accommodations.

"Oh, you guys and girls, give me something to do at 9:15 pm," Mr. Hawthorne chuckled, finding the camper's flash light. Before hitting the switch for the outdoor light, Mr. Hawthorne clicked the portable one to make a small beam to guide his way back to the house.

"Lights out," he told the crew, "tomorrow is another day."

Coming back up the small path to the metal gate, Mr. Hawthorne looked at Jeb and George, who were holding onto to the metal wiring that was in a pentagon shape.

"It is time for bed, you two," and with one loud screech from the both the monkeys, Mr. Hawthorne was able to douse the flashlight to replace it with the traditional drive way one that led him back in the house.

Interviewing Credible Sources

Despite not having a national championship except for when Eddie Patrick performed his special feat a second time representing New Jersey, Southern Dominican Catholic University benefitted when it was documented as the institution where Eddie was studying.

"Hi, Peter," the nursing student came into the office from her daily schedule.

"Well, well, you said Dr., I understand that," Peter was on the phone with his pen in hand scribbling an animated design.

"You said the gym would be in place by fall semester 1986 when I interviewed with the school in December 1983."

Taking a seat, Bobbi Barnes filed her nails, still wearing the school nursing uniform from her all day classes, "I know that was not an interview but an interview," he continued to question the higher ups.

"So, when do you think we are going to have a real gym so we can have a real athletic department?"

Peter King continued to listen as well as write down on the legal pads important words like, 'We need a gym yesterday'.

"What do you mean when is my story deadline," Peter kept the conversation, "what if I do not have a deadline?"

On that final question Peter King heard a dead line on the other end; he then saw Bobbi there ready to take five.

"I do not believe that," Peter screeched, "he just hung up."

"Are you writing a story on a sports facility?"

"No, that is not the point," Peter answered, "back when I was looking to purchase which school I was going to attend, they said there would be a gym by next fall."

Continuing to file her nails, Bobbi came to the conclusion, "How does that affect your education here at Southern Dominican Catholic University?"

"Well, ESP," Peter started to think.

"ESP what, if you had a gym here you would read other people minds?"

"Our school would attract—"

"Attract," Bobbi paused, "a lot of people who are interested in not going to class." She continued to refer to students more interested in playing games then building an intellectual body.

"They go to class."

"When?"

`"During the summer during the week." `

"They are traveling and we are a small school and focused in on academics."

As their debate continued, "Remember when we were in high school?"

"And Abigail and you loved those sporting events and I was—"

"Volunteering at the hospital," he said as she put down the nail file down and picked up the bag.

"My point being we all found our interests back then and we came here with committed goals except for Abigail," Bobbi stated, standing.

"What, she has goals?" Peter defended the cheerleader with model looks, "she has a skill of looking pretty and from a newspaper standpoint that is legitimate."

"That's it," Bobbi exclaimed, "her features are credible but she needs to go to class to understand how to use those skills in the proper fashion."

"And she does."

"Yeah, I am very happy about that," Bobbi agreed.

Holding the door, Bobbi entered into the dark hallway that was now empty during the off hours, "So, where do you want to go for dinner?"

"Is that all you think about is food?"

Continuing Education

Unlike other barns that could school into the night with lights and an indoor ring, the small circular dirt area with a large green outdoor pasture right next to it worked out fine for the college students working their skills.

"Oh, how I miss walking on the trails with The Great Satan," Danielle Lynne hinted to Eddie Patrick who transferred to a nice training center for the disabled when he was in high school instead of the backyard stable where 'Special Person to Ride' started. Today, at County Line Stables, they had a home like atmosphere despite not a trail in sight. To go on a trail ride, they had hauled out the truck with the twin portable stalls and wheeled it down to a nearby Gator Glades Park where schooling shows took precedence.

Looking up from his mount, Eddie noticed the innocent preppie image in Danielle Lynne's eyes as she walked around the dirt track on the other side of the rail with a feed bucket.

"Why don't you do another trot and over at the tree break into a canter?" hearing her suggestion, Eddie did not breathe a word; instead, with a small cluck The Great Satan woke up from his relaxing walk and picked up the speed. Watching very closely, Danielle Lynne observed Eddie's body go up and down then up again.

There was weakness there and there was strength, she thought to herself as they crept closer to the tree that was acting like a marker.

Since Eddie was a national champion at the walk, a discipline known as dressage was something Eddie had an understanding of despite not doing really hard like the able-bodied tests. Instead, this education prepared him for the transition at the tree. Keeping his eyes up, Eddie concentrated very hard on what was in front and his corner eye picked up where that tree was and as they came closer he pulled the outside reign then clicked. And hearing this command, the fiery chestnut picked up the rocking horse motion, which allowed Eddie the opportunity to just sit back.

"His back is getting straighter, Uncle Nate," she noted to her uncle.

"That it is."

Eddie could feel the hard tension in his once spastic arms as they slightly touched the saddle's pommel and were very still like a classic equestrian ballet dancer would have them when being judged.

"Looking really good, Eddie," Danielle Lynne shouted as The Great Satan kept his circular corners near the rail, which really impressed the trainer, showing that he was aware of that concept.

"Next time at the tree, why don't you come back to a walk and cool down."

Once again, without a sound, Eddie waited to feel his shoulder come aligned with the tree when he slightly pulled back on The Great Satan's mouth, which was the signal that it was time to slow down to rest. When the pair returned to the area that had Danielle Lynne finishing putting the feed in the buckets, she mentioned the fact that he went deep in the ring's corners that were circular.

"Well, our shows are patterned after regular horse shows and we learn to go into the corners," Eddie exclaimed, still riding The Great Satan with a loose reign, "and the dressage tests are the same, which means I learned the basics back in New Jersey."

"Oh yeah, that is right," she remembered, which made her think that not only was he a couple thousand miles from home but was making strides in an area where nobody knew who he was due to the fact he studied something seriously back home.

Horse Communication

"Why do you braid a horse's mane?"

"I do not know, it takes time and there is nothing to hold onto when you go into a three point position."

"Nothing to hold onto could be the point," Mischa answered her friend as they experimented with New Hope's handle bars, "but you're supposed to trust your mount as you work together to accomplish whatever you're trying to accomplish in the show ring."

Autumn Taylor shot back from the step stool that Eddie Patrick used to get on The Great Satan.

"That's true," Autumn agreed, "but have you noticed in the movies the girls have hair that is all over the place, I mean even Jessica McCord when she takes the helmet and hair net off her hair is all over the place."

"And why do you think Jessica Mc Cord has a hair net underneath her helmet?"

"To keep her shiny perfect hair all clean for her next modeling shoot."

"Yeah, look at me and my horse," Autumn played with the conversation, "and of course this beautiful housing development."

"Hey, that housing development has our horse shows that we can afford."

"Hay is for horses, ain't that right, New Hope?" Autumn answered while New Hope sneezed.

"Ain't is not a word."

"Ain't that the truth," Autumn cracked back, finishing the job, "Mr. Hawthorne, I am going to ride New Hope with a braided mane."

"Hello, you two," Mr. Hawthorne said after Eddie Patrick pulled his non air-conditioned automobile into the grassy parking space that has no lines only; Jeb and George greeting them with a screech.

With great curiosity, the two characters latched onto the shapely wire and could listen in on the conversation if they were quiet.

"We have a fundraiser to go to," Mr. Hawthorne announced, "a local organization wants to have an evening auction of South Florida memorabilia including a dress worn on the boat of that model that had the tryst with the politician."

"Oh yeah, I remember that," Danielle Lynne mentioned, "It was in all the papers."

Fun Raising Questions

Like friendly neighbors, Jeb and George screeched their approval and Eddie Patrick, with a cane in each hand, brought up the question.

"How much are the tickets?"

"Only twenty dollars," Mr. Hawthorne answered, "I figure we can go as a barn together."

"That is a great idea," Danielle Lynne added.

As New Hope stuck his head out the stall door with a mane that looked like it just came back from the beautician, the two kid grooms came running up the path to unlock the metal gate.

"Mr. Hawthorne, Autumn is going to ride New Hope with braids on."

"She is," he turned his attention to the youngster. "You have to learn how to grip them," Danielle Lynne interjected, going back to being Miss Danielle Lynne from a college student.

As Mischa looked at her small hand and thought about the question, Autumn joined the trio who were chatting at the top of the hill near the monkey cage.

"C'mon, Mischa," Autumn said putting on her black gloves, "New Hope is ready to go, oh, hi, Miss Danielle Lynne and National Champion, oh sorry, Miss Olympian."

Returning to their conversation, Mr. Hawthorne continued to discuss the evening that featured raising the money for the club.

"I think it is a great idea," and Danielle Lynne shook her head positively to Eddie Patrick's statement.

"Well, we have a planning meeting at Flamingo Hospital tomorrow night, would you two be able to join us?"

"I do not have any class tomorrow night, do you, Eddie?"

"No, we can be there."

Writing and Acting, Acting and Writing

Making her way through the second semester, the first week was bearable for Bobbi Barnes, who was snacking on a soda and chocolate bar wearing a business style suit. It was not a work day and this did not have anything to do with class; instead, the classroom assignment stated was to wear a 'dress for success' look and go to Flamingo Hospital and sit inside the cafeteria or another place where patients' families can relax then write a two page essay on your feelings about the experience.

Bobbi found this to be very strange on the same level as being having theater class as a requirement to the degree. After taking the stage credit on a pass or fail basis, the nursing student decided to take those notes from the first semester freshman year and apply them to this situation. Like watching a thespian working a character on stage, she people watched the action that was happening in the hospital setting.

Throughout the hour sitting that included the power food, there seemed to be constant flow of workers coming into the break area while only a few costumers to the health care business. Wearing white jackets, it seemed the young girl who wore her whites with pride saw the action using an objective critical eye in the same way Peter would over at the community youth baseball games.

It seemed the emergency room or the individuals working in areas that needed to have a sanitized atmosphere were ones utilizing the food services. Unlike floors above her, the dressing was on the very casual level due to the constant messy situations they would encounter during their business days.

Finding ice in the plastic container, Bobbi started to remember back to the time her father used to bring in ice chips that had the same small crackly size that was left from the soda.

'The cold something to do feeling', brightened her spirits while spending two hours watching hospital related soap operas.

Chomping on the chips inside the paper cup, thinking of the memories made, the thoughts a little stronger walking down the hallway. Taking more mental notes had the characters around her doing things in their own world. A couple people said 'hello' to the college student who shed her uniform for an outfit that would be more suited for an office job interview.

But why would I want to work in a controlled situation, she thought opening the door, *instead, everything was different on the floor.*

Behind her, sounds could be heard in Spanish and she ignored the comments, walking to the car that was parked in the lot across the driveway. Thinking about it, the assignment did work and was not a waste of time. In fact, observing the hour and going home to report about what she saw brought together different skills that assisted in understanding the profession she was making a commitment to at Southern Dominican Catholic University.

Space for Raising Fun Questions

Inside his dorm room that was unlike Eddie's living space, Peter planted his SDCU relaxing time in a place where somebody would get a few winks of sleep. Turning his attention to the open door, the reporter observed Eddie's dirty boots and two canes pound his way through the carpeted hallway.

Noticing not even a dust molecule on the dresser, Peter followed his friend down the corridor to his door. Pulling his keys off his belt buckle, Eddie stuck the key into the lock.

"Boo," Peter interjected, the word while grabbing when he scared Eddie, "sorry, I didn't mean to knock you over."

"Yes, you did."

"Well, that is true," Peter said, watching the door open to the room which consisted of a bed with a sheet half off.

Since the twice a month maid service did not come by for another couple days, Eddie's living space had the appearance of being lived in regularly. Twice a month maid service to all the dorm rooms was the Sisters' idea and it killed two birds with one stone. Extra money for the local motel workers and the semi clean areas made for better studying conditions. But Eddie still felt very confined in his room that was smaller than the hourly rate facilities down the street that the Sisters believed serviced the truckers as they came to the end of the Interstate.

No matter how hard Peter tried, they would drive down Biscayne Boulevard to do a count and the Sisters' intuition was right; the motels in the area had a gold mine for the trucking industry. For a low cost there was a shower and a couple hours sleep in a bed that was comfortable after the three day trip.

"You off to the library tonight?"

"Yup, going to take a shower and head up there to catch up on some assignments."

"How did practice go today?" the school paper editor, who did mostly sports, asked his friend in a supportive fashion.

"Fine, in fact, we are going to have a fundraiser, an auction of memorabilia including the dress worn in the political tryst down at the Miami docks."

"Oh yeah, Gov. Boat they called it despite him not being the Governor or yeah, the other one was 'I Left My Heart in Biscayne Bay', then there was 'No Rice at This Wedding'."

"Apparently this organization has it and is willing to allow us to raise money through an auction."

"I thought they burned it."

"I guess not."

Turning the rabbit ear color television on, the news came on and it came back to him that the anchor on the local report was the same one that was on the New York City television when Eddie was lying in the hospital after surgery.

"Well, got to run," the reporter suggested and lying on the bed, staring at the ceiling, he could hear the television talk about another violent act somewhere in the city.

Some Racing Room

With a paddock area that looked like a tree lined resting area, the white bulbs were still on from the final race. Prices were still up, announcing the patron's winnings from their successful bets. Angel Damian still had the leather straps around her neck as she walked over the sacred wood chips that designated the horses walking area. Unlike a horse show, there was no place to warm up over fences; instead, in the traditional style the horses are paraded from their motel rooms on the back stretch all the way through the race track to a holding area known as the paddock. Once there, they find themselves saddled up and they meet their jockey for a quick hello followed by getting inside the tropical setting that had palm trees to create shady areas.

Feeling a little hungry, Angel Damian entered into the jockey's room where the sandwich's had some really good bread to it. Caroline Crawford used to call it

'Wonder' but it seemed to have a soft texture that made the salad that was put into pretty good.

"Wow...," said the one jockey who was applying aftershave before getting his gear to go home, "an exercise rider in the jockey's room and another Caroline Crawford prototype."

"By the end of the meet, I will have my license and next year watch out, also, I do not look anything like Caroline Crawford, I am good looking," the former show rider joked.

Something was said in Spanish that Angel decided to ignore while going to the counter.

"You know, you need a license to sit at this counter, Miss Angel?"

"But the backstretch closed down for the night," Angel squeaked like the teenager she was and tried to milk an inexpensive meal.

Holding her car keys in her hand, Caroline Crawford entered into the scene, "It is good to be the leader of the pack."

Under her breath, the teenage exercise girl, who used to win blue ribbons on the backstretch when the races were dark, said, "Pack of what?"

In true power play tradition, Caroline heard the comment and fluffed her fake leather jacket, "Leading jockey, preppie."

Wondering whether the comment was a complement, razzing, or sign of hatred, Angel Damian accepted her food in a bag then turned around, "Preppie I am and I learned how to ride a horse," then changing her speech pattern, "not ride a horse."

"You have your fences and I have my barrels."

"And I have grace while you only have speed."

As the others in the room who could understand their conversation stood around, they could be heard saying the word 'muchachas' a couple times in the sentence, waiting with their pesos patiently for the fists to fly.

But the eye contact was only theatrical, "Cannot wait until the license is approved."

A Picture is Worth a Million Memories

As the South Florida Sunshine glistened, Calfee sat there with the book while tending waiting for people to come by to order paintings and sculptures from the show class that he observed then created.

"Straw, what does the words 'to benefit' mean?"

"They are the ones receiving money from holding the competition?"

"I guess that is what makes it newsworthy and not just a bunch of people riding horses over fences."

"Ah, yes, an organization gets their name connected with people socializing with their horses on a Sunday afternoon, interesting concept."

There was a sound coming from Straw's trailer and the elderly gentlemen stood up to go into the make shift dark room.

"Good morning, Mr. Calfee," said a young child wearing her blue blazer really tight with a string tied at its button.

"You here to show horses?" he asked her as she perused the catalog of sculptures that he could send out from the home base.

"I like this one," the young girl paused, "Mommy."

Remembering that this was winter break up north, Straw bit his tongue since the kindergarten first grader was a customer.

"Hello, Calfee," the mother said, "is she bothering you at all?"

"No, I made these to be looked at," he replied.

"We are from South Carolina."

"Spending the vacation learning to be an Equestrian."

"Checking out a few ponies today, then going back to the beach."

"So you are doing a favor for someone on your day off from vacation?"

"She looks really good on the one she is showing today and they are very good in the competition."

"Well, that is a good thing."

Coming out of next door trailer, Straw held a wet picture that was finishing developing, "Look what I have here," he said.

"Look, Mommy, it is the white horse I rode earlier," the young girl screeched, running to Straw's vendor booth.

Smiling, the mother opened her pocket book, "Ten dollars and I have a frame."

Pulling out a twenty, the mother gave it to Straw while the young girl already had the whole still photo in her small hands.

"Well, that is a nice souvenir to take back home, hon," the little girl's mother stated.

Giving back the change, Straw smirked at her, "You cannot get at other tourist destination gift shops."

Walking away, the older man could hear the little girl verbally exchange wither her mother, "Was he talking about the expensive place that has the mouse?"

"Yeah, that is an expensive place to go just to have fun."

"I guess that class benefited that little girl," Calfee continued the conversation.

"Yup," Straw replied, "made her look really good to have her picture taken."

Schooling for a Course

Unlike some of her time in high school, Danielle Lynne was not on winter break, sitting in the bleachers, watching them set up a course in a class where she could earn points to qualify for a National Championship. Instead, the jumping combination that she was encountering for an hour today had to deal with staying awake during a one-sided discussion about how the mind works. Taking down notes on a legal pad worked in the same way as walking the fences studying each stride and figuring out how many to perform in between each obstacle.

Printed on the text book the word 'Introduction' stated the first $29.95 investment in this commitment will only be profitable if the words inside were read and understood. In the back, there were questions while definitions were highlighted throughout the chapters dropping hints there were the words that needed to be memorized.

According to the syllabus, there were supposed to be quizzes every Friday to check if you were keeping up with the logical thinking that some in the class would grasp while others will find themselves buying another 'Introductory' reading material inside the corporate owned bookstore.

"As I close this lecture, remember it is not important to spit back the definitions to the words in Chapter One instead, understand what the concept of the word is, is that clear to everybody?"

Standing up, the group of people murmured and Professor McCoombs flipped her chalk. Walking out the door, the Equestrian, who was well-known around the horses, had her casual shorts on, making her way through the mass of bodies that will disappear within minutes.

Academics is Really Elementary

Waving her hand, Mrs. Taylor saw Autumn standing right next to Mischa in the elementary school parking lot. As the car came close to the curb, Autumn quickly reached for the door when it came to the stop.

"Mom."

"Yes," Mrs. Taylor turned her head to the backseat.

"We need to go to the library."

Mrs. Taylor knew that today was not a barn day instead, studies took over the grammar school pair's schedule. "So, what are you two going to do at the library?"

"Mrs. Davis wants us to complete a one page writing assignment."

"When did Mrs. Davis assign this assignment?"

"Today," Autumn said underneath her breath but Mrs. Taylor smiled.

"Okay, I will drop you off and is an hour enough time?"

"Yeah," Autumn said underneath her breath and Mrs. Taylor smiled, hearing every word.

Backpacks over the shoulders, the two made it through the main lobby where there were announcements of area activities along with different things for growing children. Feeling intimidated, they bypassed adult library and headed into children's section which was smaller than the big people's. Despite the size, the same exact fact finding mission rules applied and straight across the room to the card index the two put in their strategy to attack the job that needs to be done to accomplish a good grade.

"Who was Christopher Columbus?" Mischa asked her friend.

"He discovered America," said Autumn who knew that since her name reflected the season that came with the holiday.

"No, he did not discover America, America Vespoopie discovered America."

Starting to giggle, the librarian came across the room to the pair and put her glasses on like she was a judge at a horse show.

"Can I help you two?" she inquired.

"We are looking for a book about Christopher Columbus, the person who discovered America," Mischa responded.

"Are you sure the Vikings didn't discover America?" the out-of-school teacher questioned as they flipped the cards in the small brown box.

"That is a football team," the girls gleamed back.

"And where does that football team play?" she asked.

"Where it snows," Mischa came back.

"And where is that?"

"Up north," Autumn continued the conversation.

"In America," Mischa followed the deduction like it was going from a single combination to a double with their horse.

"And put the word together," the librarian helped them.

"North," Autumn started, "America," Mischa followed.

"North America," the two said in unison like a horse rider combination going over a fence.

"Yes, the Vikings discovered North America."

Autumn kept her fingertips inside the card number and found what she was looking for, "This one sounds good."

"Do you know where you are going?" the librarian checked.

Seeing the proper call numbers that were listed on the card, she told the helper, "Yup, I know exactly where I am going, Mr. Dewey,"

"Not Hewey and Louie," Mischa followed Autumn's lead.

"No, Mr. Dewey, the decimal system will guide me to the proper place in the library to get what I need."

With all that said, the librarian backed off and went back to her desk to check the return books and she was really impressed while watching Autumn and Mischa know exactly what they were doing inside the area of self-taught education.

He disappeared in between aisles then reappearing with each carrying a book about Christopher Columbus.

"This one is for you, Mischa, and this one is for me," Autumn took control of the situation.

Sitting down at a very small table for adults, the kids opened the books to start to read.

"Autumn, this book says Christopher Columbus discovered the West Indies," Mischa reported.

"But this one says he discovered America; which one says American Fettuccine discovered America?"

"Neither one, shoot," Mischa admitted, feeling like she lost a bet.

Checking her watch, Autumn was reminded that her mother was going to be picking them up in a few minutes. And they picked up the books and walked over to the librarian who was there to help. Handing them the cards, the librarian checked them out and told them when to bring them back.

"That is all right," Autumn said, "the assignment is due tomorrow so we will have the books real soon."

After finding their ways out the door just like in the school parking lot, Autumn had her hand in the air.

Exploring a New World

"Monsters were in the ocean, they all thought, but somebody took a minute to look beyond that obstacle to find the new world," the cheerleader typed into her computer and popped the big square disk out of the drive. Shutting off the black-and-white monitor that actually had green lettering, Abigail left her dorm room, finally completing the elementary education assignment that was to write an essay about a historical figure explaining how facts as well as opinions can be applied to modern life.

In reality, like the performer that she was, Abigail grabbed the first thing that came into her mind and ran with the idea. Christopher Columbus and his deal with the Queen of Spain was an easy target for the one page homework due next class. Now that it was done, she put her sneakers back on and grabbed the Walkman from inside the drawer.

Heading out into the darkness, she started to ponder about what she scribed for the 'three days a week' commitment that was supposed to develop her preliminary skills or give her taste of Education Major. *Monsters were in the ocean and everybody thought that the world was flat.*

It sounded logical; you walk around on a relatively flat surface, Abigail concluded, heading out the door to break into an eighties style jog, *but the reality is like a big blue marble; the earth was round without any pointy edges to it.*

Coming up to the mall, she slowed a bit to look down the alley that was lined with palm trees and at its doorstep was the chapel all lit up. Raising her head, she noticed the bell tower with the cross at its peak.

Having a little bit of sweat on her, Abigail approached the doors shining in the manila white lights. Slowly, they opened and there was the half-naked man on the pulleys laying on two pieces of wood with a look of distress.

One person took a minute to look beyond the obstacle to find a new world.

Surf Report

Hearing the surf from outside the apartment that Mr. Walt set her up in, Angel Damian enjoyed the soft texture bread that had the roast beef inside it. Before leaving the track, the exercise rider picked up the *Racing Form* from the overnight news stand and was studying the next day's card. Not to bet instead, she was monitoring the times and distances of the athletic horses who only knew how to run.

On the television, which Mr. Walt wired up with cable, the South Florida news was on and the sports section was very quiet since it was not football season. In about a month, the baseball teams will be down with spring training while clips from other cities filled the winter night's report. Finally, the announcer said, "Another proposal for a new football stadium has been shot down," he said, "so, when is there going to be another facility to replace the one we have now?"

"And, most importantly, where are we going to stick this one, wouldn't kill them to play the games on the beach then the tourists wouldn't have to leave the surf to catch the game, that is it for tonight."

Angel Damian just chuckled, trying to find worthwhile information inside tomorrow's seventh race past performances. Deciding the night's work was complete she closed the industry publication and walked out to the balcony that was lined with other rooms.

She could see the white in the distance and could hear the crackling of the water hitting the sand. It came and it went immediately then it came again just to instantly leave like the natural actions of the ocean at the beach.

Going past to the aquatic end point, or where it decides to turn around, Angel Damian only saw darkness on the backdrop knowing that her future was just like that and the mysterious thought made her energized.

Communicating Artistically

Something came over her that exchanged the perspiration from the evening exercise to a more spiritual stimulation. Going into one of the pews, she found herself without any thoughts about tests or assignments, only a feeling of being under a comforter on a cold winter night.

Above her was the artistic sculpture featuring a shirtless man who was not wearing any shoes nailed to pieces of wood in the hands and feet. For some this image sometimes had meaning who prayed to a concept that someone captured in a vision inspired by the written word.

They thought there were monsters in the ocean, Abigail, wearing an A on her necklace, thought, *and those storytellers thought he was the son of God,* she pointed at the cross.

All they had were dreamers back then who decided to tell things through storytelling and tales that seemed unbelievable. "And it took one man in each story with a conflict to look beyond to discover a new world."

From the back of the church, Abigail could hear something, "And those who sacrifice things, Muff, not as martyrs instead, educators so others can learn are the ones who are gifted in this world."

"Eddie," Abigail said turning her head.

"No, it is not Eddie, it's Peter," was the response.

"Peter, my name is not Muffy, it is Abigail, see the 'A' on my necklace."

"Yeah, yeah, the A on the Cracker Jack box jewelry."

Abigail let the comment slide and Peter took a seat next to her in the pew, "Such an interesting story the sculpture tells. You know they did not have cameras back then and reporters."

"I remember doing a homework assignment when I was a little girl in Catholic school: if I was a reporter on Good Friday, what type of story would I write."

"So did I."

Sitting back in the pew was replaced with Peter kneeling, making the sign of the cross while Abigail just watched him then deflected her eyes toward the sculpture that brought them to peace.

When the journalist was finished, he sat back in the pew and the two continued their thoughts not making a sound.

"What do you think, Peter?"

"What do you mean?" he answered the question with a question.

"Why are we here, praying?"

"To take a few moments to ponder on things and have a chit chat with God."

"Do you think he talks back through that water over there?" Abigail noted the running water that had a soothing voice to it as it filled the Holy Water basin.

"That is a good point," said the reporter who observed and broke things down into an understanding then put it into words agreed.

"You know," Abigail continued the whisper, "he was a teacher."

"Yup."

"And so was St. Newman, he cared for the kids."

"Now, how do you know that?" Peter questioned.

"The Sisters, when I first arrived here during orientation, showed me that statue over there of the man teaching the children," she reported, "it was a gift for the Education Department, the Stations of the Cross is for the Nursing Department."

Looking around, Peter did not see anything of the communication department that he was a student in as a journalist.

"You know why there are no names on the buildings?"

"No, why, Abigail?" noticing the soon-to-be Education major was picking up some interesting information.

"The Sisters thought instead of putting the names on the buildings which serve no real purpose besides confusing the students on their first days," Abigail conversed to Peter.

Now turning his attention back to the cross, Peter quietly spoke, "Now I know why we need a gym and a studio bigger than a shoe box."

Abigail broke into a giggle, which made them both laugh showing emotion as the exchanged thoughts to each other.

Standing up, Abigail bent her knee as did Peter when the two left the pew and before leaving each went over to the babbling brook that was running with the water that talked in a very spiritual way.

Taking a finger, they both took a drop and placed it on their forehead before making the cross again.

"I guess this is when we tell God we got the message."

Cost of Living

"Age old question is a fundraiser about making money or educating the public," Eddie pondered once again with one of those legal pads in front of him.

Both hands had the wrist bands covering the scars from that bad night and the quick decision that ended up as a just a cry for help since nurses did their jobs making sure he was a priority.

"Age old question is a fundraiser making money or educating the public," Eddie Patrick scribbled on the legal pad and Danielle Lynne giggled.

As the proposal was delivered about memorabilia being used to as a selling point create a bottom line to survive, Danielle Lynne leaned close to Eddie Patrick.

"So, what is therapeutic horseback riding?"

In the same way, a power was unleashed when Abigail and Peter placed the water from the babbling brook inside the church on their forehead, the electricity seemed stimulating when a friend asked Eddie Patrick that question.

Quiet Please

Only a few floors above the meeting, Bobbi Barnes was seated at the nurse's station with a pen in hand, fulfilling her part time duties that in a couple years she hoped would be a full time career.

Down the hallway, patients slept some with machines and others just getting through the one sheet evening on the bare essentials. Doing paperwork and homework at the same time, Bobbi cherished the night's hours of peace.

Why do you think the Sisters put me in this situation? she thought, walking the lonely hallways that only had patient's beds lining it like a hotel without the enmities. Granted the textbooks were words that they had to study but this was not in reading material. There was no one there only individuals restricted to a bed resting, grabbing a blood pressure machine she proceeded to do her job.

Already having the thermometer in her pocket, she slowly walked into the dark room. Making her way into the blackness from the yellowish-orange, Bobbi did not even think about hitting the light switch.

"Excuse me," the student nurse whispered, "it is time to take the blood pressure and temperature."

"I had just fallen asleep."

"Sorry," Bobbi apologized and she could hear the phone at the station ring.

Enjoying Each Other's Company

After the meeting, Mr. Hawthorne went north on the Interstate while Eddie and Danielle Lynne drove around the block where the school was located. Before turning into the college campus, they decided to make a pit stop for dinner at an Italian restaurant that catered to the students. It was a really nice place with low cost subs and due to the dry campus establishment, it acted as a civil escape for the age group being tested across the street.

"You never told me," Danielle Lynne handed the menu after ordering, "what really is therapeutic horseback riding?"

With the canes on the ground, Eddie Patrick sat in the chair just like anybody else did when two people went out to dinner together to share thoughts in a relaxing place.

"What is therapeutic horseback riding?" he answered with a question.

For two summers, he trained to be the nation's best in one class and when reporters came out the second time around, they did not ever ask him what exactly it was instead like the high kicking Christmas show in New York City. The story was a simple observation that really did not need explaining.

"It is my sport," he responded, feeling that urge to compete with the baseball team, "and it is something that I win at."

"I guess I win at it too," Danielle Lynne replied, "and if there is winning, it must be a sport."

After all those isolated high school years and the busy one called the freshman, Eddie found it refreshing to sit down and talk to somebody about a common interest.

199

Granted during last semester and Christmas break there were social times while this simple subject never came up.

"I guess it was the fundraiser that sprang the question," Danielle Lynne, who was now working with a Psychology line on course, informed Eddie, never feeling comfortable about the money thing and was very grateful the opportunities that the concept offered him which in reality were on the same lines as the division two athlete he competed with in the classroom.

"It will be a fun night out," Eddie continued the conversation as the waitress picked up the garlic roll basket which now had small puddles on the paper.

"That was good," Danielle Lynne went back to being a friend on a college let's pick something to eat out night.

"The garlic rolls?" was the response, "Peter and I used to get them delivered to the newsroom last year."

"You all seem to be good friends."

"I guess you can say that."

Eddie met Peter during a freshmen orientation class and it was the local hanging out with his community friends, which included Bobbi Barnes the nursing student. Peter was the one making comical jokes throughout the introductory to college shtick that was a required course for everybody pass/fail. After the fifty minutes, the group invited him to lunch and it made Eddie feel a little bit more comfortable on campus.

The two equestrians split the check and while walking out Danielle Lynne opened door, "So, are you going to ask me to this fundraiser?"

And Eddie Patrick looked at her giving her a smile.

Dressing for Success

They were in the bathroom after a long day of riding, but now it was time to look pretty since Eddie and his friend invited them to go to a fundraiser.

"Mischa, what is the term just a friend?" Autumn asked, looking in the mirror.

"Just a friend is just a friend," Mischa answered back.

In the other bedroom to the small cottage that was sleeping quarters for riders who were very dedicated or had nothing to go home to, Mr. Hawthorne stood in front of his mirror staring into it thinking about the past.

"She had a great white jumper, yes, she did," Mr. Hawthorne thought back to the junior rider who really made him stay enthusiastic about this activity that captured his heart. Granted she moved onto better pastures, "Uncle Nate," the call came from the kitchen and Danielle Lynne's eye caught the colorful memories that lined the trophy case with the picture of the white jumper that had a mysterious rider aboard taking a fence at the national horse show in New York City.

"Who was she, Uncle Nate?" the question came that made him turn around to come back to reality.

"She went onto better pastures," he just said, "she was a wonderful rider and we used to go at it for points when we were younger. And then…"

"She found better pastures."

"Yeah, she went on to better pastures."

"That looks nice," his niece stated while the two ten-year-olds came out from the makeup room looking like fourteen year olds.

"Do we look nice, presentable?" Autumn asked.

"Does it look like our boots are polished and we are waiting at the in gate?" Mischa added to the need to have a 'my feelings stroked' moment.

With his tie straightened from his niece's assistance, Mr. Hawthorne took one look at his squad, "Yes, you all look nice. And we are going to this fundraiser as a barn, a small barn but—"

"Uncle Nate, it is not quantity, it is quality," Danielle Lynne reassured him that everything was going to be all right.

As a foursome, the troupe walked through the kitchen then out the door, where a yellow light shined on Eddie Patrick who was waiting at the door.

"What are you thinking?" Danielle Lynne asked as the kids passed by Eddie and Uncle Nate shut the door.

"It is nice we are all going out as a barn."

Working Together

Passing by Eddie's dorm room door, Peter concluded that he was not there and continued through the main hallway where the security guard was checking a couple freshman identification cards.

With a blue tint to the swimming pool, the editor to the school paper watched the lights go off and the isolated area go dark. Following the lighted sidewalk to his car, he hopped in and started the engine.

Driving through the 'bad neighborhood', Peter found himself in the left lane to the hospital. As the emergency vehicle cut him off with the bright lights, the reporter yielded then followed it into the parking lot. Slowing down, the speed o' meter read 15 mph and he saw Bobbi Barnes with a hiking back pack on her shoulders. Pulling into the half circle, the car stopped and she opened the door, "Thanks for picking me up."

"It is Saturday night."

"Well, I am a nurse and that is what it is."

"And I am a reporter," he told her, her lip touching his cheek.

"Well, thank you."

As the driver who communicated with the mass public by writing made a right hand turn to take the light, the health care worker who talked to people on an individual basis asked a question.

"Where are Danielle Lynne and Eddie tonight?"

When she asked the question, it reminded Peter that tonight was the big fundraiser.

"Oh, that is right, tonight was their fundraiser," he said, engaging through the bad part of town in the car.

"Why didn't you go?"

Arriving at the school, he found a space and threw the gear into the park position.

"Maybe Gimpy did not buy me a ticket."

"That is a good reason," Bobbi responded, "so, what are we going to do tonight?"

Peter smirked and she looked at him starting to laugh, "Nah."

"Yeah."

"Which hotel."

"The Lauderdale Clipper."

"Nah, it will never work."

"Yeah it will," Peter answered, moving the gear into reverse.

Having Fun Raising Money

Only a couple tables were sold out and the veteran rider and trainer Nathaniel Hawthorne expected that result. Looking around, his contingents who surrounded their table had a smile that showed his barn still supported each other in positive ways.

"Mr. Hawthorne?"

"Yes, Autumn?"

"This organization invited you here."

"They are raising money for us and the special kids who ride at the farm."

"So we can build the barn?"

Danielle Lynne knotted her head, "Yes, so the horses have place to go in the rain."

"Oh."

Since owning the farm, Nathaniel Hawthorne came to the conclusion that despite only having a couple stalls, in true honesty the horses enjoyed living out doors and not cramped up in a stall. With the South Florida weather being nearly perfect, every day the stalls would be a trapped existence for them.

"Before we start the auction, I would like to take a brief moment to give some acknowledge to the person who brought us here tonight, owner of County Line Stables, Nathaniel Hawthorne," the man behind the podium said, "every weekend Nathaniel Hawthorne opens up his barn on Saturday morning so children with disabilities can ride."

Danielle Lynne smiled, knowing Eddie Patrick's story by heart and remembering that the horse was a very caring animal that will do anything to help out.

"So Eddie," Danielle Lynne whispered a question, "what is therapeutic horseback riding?"

Eddie heard the question but continued to concentrate on the presentation like a student sitting at a desk in the classroom. And some television show trinkets from the South Florida production seemed to collect a couple dollars from the tables that seemed to be filled by the organization's executive board.

"Well, they're picking up a couple bucks," Uncle Nate told his niece while lighting his pipe.

"Shh, Uncle Nate, it is for a worthy cause," Danielle Lynne chuckled.

"Yes, I run a worthy cause," he smiled, looking straight at Eddie who started to do the math.

As the evening progressed and it seemed the executive board was doing some winter Christmas shopping, both Autumn and Mischa were toying with the colorful ice cream that they were comparing to the one that they ate at the awards banquet right before the holiday.

"This one is better, Mischa," Autumn reported.

"Nah, I think they taste the same."

At that moment, the organization brought out a seductive looking dress that was worn in a political tryst. All of a sudden, Eddie could feel his leg get kicked and when he turned around, Danielle Lynne gave him the 'well bid on it dew fish' glare.

Putting his hand up the barns, the national champion was following orders from the stable's equestrian wanting to be an Olympian.

Someone on the executive board stared back with the 'what is a college student doing bidding on a dress worn in a political tryst'. In the next minute, Eddie raised another fist and the rest of the room looked back at the executive board member who decided to give up since the television stuff was going to be a headache getting to the car.

"It is only a dress worn in a political tryst," his wife told him, patting his knuckles.

A Gem Photo of a Tryst

Standing behind the door, Peter had his lens cap off with the telephoto piece snapped on to the main unit. Watching Eddie be presented with the dress, the reporter snapped the image so it could be saved forever and remembered as the event of being presented with a dress from a political tryst actually happened.

"Did you get the shot?" Bobbi whispered like Danielle Lynne did a couple minutes before at the table. When Eddie returned to his seat, there was applause and everybody started to stand up.

"I guess it is over," Peter said, backing off the doorway and the two scurried to a safer location.

Tying the sweater around her shoulders, Danielle Lynne left the ball room and turned to Eddie, "I am getting cold."

Just like earlier, Eddie heard the comment but did not return a response, noticing Peter and Bobbi sitting on the chairs in the lobby.

"Hey, what are you guys doing here?"

"Gimpy forgot to buy me a ticket."

"Us, you and Eddie forgot to buy us a ticket." Bobbi swung her nurse's finger with a laugh.

"Sorry about that, you two," Eddie responded.

"So, was the food good?"

Whatever tension was there had been released and Danielle Lynne saw her Uncle Nate putting an envelope into his pocket when he arrived at the group.

"Uncle Nate, this is my roommate and her friend," the Jersey Girl introduced the strangers.

"Yes, Hi, Peter and Bobbi; how is everything going at the school?"

"It is going fine."

"Hey, Peter, my brother won his stock car division last week at the dirt track," Mischa interjected the remark, "is that news for your section?"

And Autumn watched Peter with an interesting eye.